SWEET LITTLE LIES

(SIGNED WITH A KISS, BOOK 1)

JESSICA SORENSEN

 Created with Vellum

1

ALEXIS

I started to wonder if people can break on the inside but remain completely put together on the outside. Not that I believe I'm put together on the outside. No, I can be a hot mess. But I don't care about how my hair is styled or if the clothes I wear are trendy.

I'm not really talking about clothes or hair, though. I'm talking about the people who appear to have it all together, like nothing can bother them, as if they can handle *anything*. And it's always in their faces. That indifference. That I-don't-give-a-shit-about-anything look in their eyes. Just glancing at them, you'd think they had fantastic lives. But really, can you tell that just from looking at someone? I used to believe so. I used to believe everyone showed who they are.

I also used to be really naïve.

Not anymore.

Now I understand that people wear masks to conceal what's really going on inside. I have my own on now, and I wear it all the time. It's not sparkly or pretty but created from a neutral mask of indifference. When I put it on, no one can see underneath it. No one can see the pain crawling around inside me, underneath my skin. Which when I really think about it makes me seem really weird.

"Oh God, here we go again," my friend Masie says from the lounge chair across from mine, drawing me from my thoughts. It's the start of spring break, and she has decided that we need to spend a lot of time hanging out and tanning. Not that I can actually tan without burning. "Seriously, Lex, you need to just tell him how you feel."

I blink at her. "What the hell are you talking about?"

She gives me a tolerant look. "I know you were thinking about Blaine. You always are whenever you get that look on your face."

In her simple statement, my point is proven—my mask is hiding everything inside me. All my dark thoughts. My emotions. My pain. Who I am now versus who I used to be.

"Sorry, but sometimes I can't help thinking about him," I lie, readjusting my sunglasses.

It's not like I don't sometimes think of Blaine. I do. Just not as much as Masie thinks I do. But there's a good reason why she believes that.

Blaine has been my friend for years, and I've had a crush on him that dates back past what I like to refer to as Before, which is the time when my parents were still alive.

Everything that happened after that, I refer to as Nothing, because that's how it feels. Like nothing matters anymore, except for a few small things that I haven't let go of yet.

Blaine is one of those things. But mostly because the way I feel about him hasn't changed.

Deep down, I know I should let go of my feelings for him; let go of him. Just let *everything* go so I can just stop feeling any goddamn thing. Become a numb shell of a person. It'll be easier that way. It's easier to feel nothing than feeling everything, like I used to. I used to let feelings own me. Control me. And it was a weakness that nearly broke me. Let them near break me.

"Why do you make everyone in school suffer by having to look at your ugly face?" Jay, one of the most popular guys in school, laughs at me.

Him and his friends are crowding around me in the hallway. It's still early enough that hardly anyone is around—thank God. The last thing I want is for someone to witness my humiliation.

"We should make you wear a paper bag over your face so no one has to look at you," he adds with a smirk as he steps toward me.

I step back even though I don't want to and wrap my arms around myself, wishing I were invisible. Wishing he hadn't noticed me. I don't know why he did and, at first, I thought he liked me, since he asked me out. But I turned him down because I'm not interested in him. I'm interested in my friend Blaine.

When I turned Jay down, he laughed in my face and told me he was only kidding but that it was cute I actually believed he wanted to go out with me. Ever since then, him and his friends have taken every opportunity to remind me of how ugly and unwanted I am.

I hate it. Hate that I'm starting off my freshman year with some of the most popular guys hating me. I don't remember Jay being this awful in middle school, but maybe he's acting this way because he has friends that are older and it makes him feel cool.

Or maybe I really am just that ugly and pathetic as they say I am.

One of Jay's friends steps up beside him and gives me an exaggerated once-over. "We should make her cover up her body, too, so we don't have to look at her gangly ass anymore."

"And her flat chest," another of Jay's friends sneers, seeming pretty pleased with himself. "Seriously, why does she even bother wearing a bra?"

Jay rubs his jawline as he muses over something. Then a wicked grin pulls at his lips. "Maybe she doesn't." He suddenly reaches for me.

Panicking, I spin to hurry away, but one of his other friends steps in front of me and blocks my path. I start to reel back around the other way when Jay grabs the back of my bra through my shirt and tugs hard. So hard the clasp snaps.

"Nope, she's actually wearing one," he sneers.

Tears burn my eyes as I wrap my arms around myself,

My eyes burn against the sunlight as the memory sears my mind. What sucks is it's not even the worst thing they did to me. I was that weak.

Not anymore, though.

I've never told anyone all the details of how deeply Jay and his friends bullied me. And they would always do it when hardly anyone was around, so reporting them was complicated. I tried a couple of times, but a lot of Jay's friends were the football stars in our school so that didn't go over well. No proof, no crime. At least, that's how our vice principal saw it.

I did confess to Masie that they were being jerks to me but never told her the entire story, partly out of embarrassment and partly because I knew she wouldn't understand. Masie has always had an easier time getting along with people and guys practically line up to date her.

She also can't seem to see me for what I really am.

Take for instance, the conversation we had a couple of years ago, right after I told her a little bit about what was going on with Jay and his friends. She had tried to convince me that the best way to get over it was to go to this pool party with her and rock a bikini so everyone would see how hot I was.

I had smiled and rolled my eyes. "There's no way in hell I'm wearing a bikini."

She sighed. "Oh, Lex, when will you start seeing things for what they really are?"

I shrug. "I do."

She sighed again. "I blame books. You read too much, and it messes with your sense of reality."

"My sense of reality is fine," I replied. Seriously, did she just say I read too much? Jesus, Masie. "And what does that even have to do with wanting to wear a bikini? Maybe it's just not my thing. Not every girl wants to wear one."

"It's not just the bikini," she said. "It's the clothes you wear. Seriously, you cover so much up. And you can be so shy sometimes. You hardly talk to people at parties. And don't even get me started on dating."

I hated when she did this, listed all my bad qualities. Sometimes I called her out on it, but that usually just let to her listed off more. "I haven't even gone on a date in a year."

"Exactly," she said, as if it proves some hidden point. "Look, we've been friends forever, so trust me when I tell you that all that shit you went through our freshman and sophomore year messed with your head. But you're not that girl anymore. You just need to realize it and start letting other people see it. You know, let your wall down or whatever."

"Aw, that's so sweet," I joked, mostly to annoy her. "But if you're about to ask me out on a date, I'm going to have to decline. Not because I don't like you and think you're not pretty; I just don't swing that way."

She sighed. "Oh, Alexis."

She said that a lot when she was frustrated with me. She

reminded me of my mom when she does it, but if I ever told her that, she'd get pissed...

I swallow hard at the thought of my mom. No matter how hard I try not to think about my parents, about the day they died, sometimes it creeps up on me.

"Earth to Alexis." Masie waves her hand in front of my face. "Did you hear anything I just said?"

I blink, forcing the memory from my thoughts.

"Um, sure," I lie, looking at her. I literally have no idea what she said.

She draws down her sunglasses and narrow her eyes at me accusingly.

I sigh. "Fine. I didn't hear you. I was just thinking about ... something."

She cocks her brow. "About Blaine?"

"No." Which is the truth, but I'm glad that's where she thinks my thoughts are. She doesn't need to know what's really going on in my head.

She rolls her eyes. "Sure you aren't."

"I'm telling the truth." I flip the page of the mystery book I've been trying to read for the last hour.

"Whatever." She rolls her eyes and slides her sunglasses back on. "You might want to put on some more sunscreen. You're starting to get a little bit pink." She glances down at her legs. "I've got an awesome tan going, though." She smirks at me. "Bet you're so jealous."

I just smile because that's what she wants me to do. Not that I don't envy her ability to get tan.

Masie is the opposite of me. Her tanned always seems to glisten and never burn. Add that to her sun-kissed blonde hair and curvy body, she's practically a beach goddess. And then there's me: long, dark brown, nearly black hair; pale skin with a few freckles here and there; tall; and slightly on the gangly side. I look like I belong in a basement or a crypt. That's okay, though. The look doesn't bother me. It might have back in the day when I used to wear a lot of pink and glittery things. But after everything, I became a new person. A person who looks like they belong in a crypt.

"A crypt?" Masie asks confusedly as she reaches for her glass of lemonade that's on the table between us.

I frown. "I didn't mean to say that aloud."

"Yeah, well, you did." She takes a sip of the drink then sets the glass down. "You know, you talk to yourself a lot."

"And you say that a lot."

"Touché." She grins.

I start to smile but frown when the back gate to her house creaks open.

Bolting upright, I reach for my towel to cover up.

"Don't you dare." Masie sits up and snatches the towel from my hands.

"Give it back," I growl, lunging at her.

Grinning, she jumps up from the lounge chair and skitters toward the diving board.

The gate is around the corner of her two-story brick house, so I don't have a view of who's coming back here. The last thing I want is for her younger brother, the pool cleaner, the landscapers, or anyone else to see me rocking these black boy short bottoms, embroidered with stars, and a matching top. My belly, legs, cleavage—what I have, anyway—and even the bottom of my ass cheeks are on display.

"Masie ..." I warn as I hurry toward her. "If you don't give me my towel back, I'll ..."

She hops onto the diving board with my towel in her hand. "You'll what?" She inches toward the edge.

"I'll ..." As panic and anger set in, I rack my brain for a vicious threat, my gaze skimming the backyard, the pool, the lounge chairs. When I spot the high-heeled, designer shoes she wore out here, an idea strikes me. I turn around. "I'll throw your shoes in the pool."

Her teasing grin fades. "You wouldn't dare."

"Wanna bet?" I pad over to the lounge chair, pick up her shoes, then walk to the edge of the pool, dangling her pretty footwear that I could never afford over the water. She knows I'll do it, too. "Now, come on; give me back my towel."

She eyes the shoes then sighs as she backs up. "Fine. But please just step away from the water. You're making me nervous."

I take a few steps back, remaining close enough in case she backs out of our agreement.

Frowning, she makes her way off the diving board and climbs down the ladder. As her feet plant on the concrete, the back-gate intruder rounds the house.

Suddenly, her younger brother, the pool boy, or the landscapers don't seem that terrible of options, because the person who enters the backyard is none other than Blaine.

Several different emotions run through me, from lust, to want, to self-consciousness. I hate that I feel this way. Hate that I still care about stuff.

As Blaine walks closer, I take in his light brown hair that's styled in a messy sort of way and his board shorts and a green shirt ...

Wait. Back the hell up. He's wearing board shorts, which means someone must have invited him over here to swim. And since this lovely, two-story, swimming pool palace belongs to only one person ...

I narrow my eyes at Masie. She flashes me an innocent look before a devious grin spreads across her face.

That little shit. She did this on purpose—invited him over right after she convinced me to wear this stupid bikini. Why, though? To humiliate me? Because that's about how I feel right now. Granted, she probably doesn't think this is humiliating. She probably believes she's doing me a favor. That if Blaine sees me in all my glorious, gangly-ass, hanging out form, we'd have one of those guy-realizes-his-best-friend-is-really-beautiful-underneath-the-punk-clothes-and-unbrushed-hair moments. That's not going to happen, though, for several reasons.

"Since when do you wear a bikini?" Blaine asks, giving me a weird, confused look.

I shrug, discreetly wrapping my arms around myself. "Masie made me wear it."

A pucker forms at his brow as his gaze sweeps up and down my body, and not in a holy-hell-she-looks-sexy way, but in a what-is-this-strange-creature-before-me way. I hug my arms tighter around myself.

"You look"—he wavers—"weird."

"I know. That's what I told Masie." I pretend to be calm, but hurt prickles through my façade, which annoys the hell out of me.

Stop feeling shit, Alexis. Just stop it. Who cares if he doesn't think you look hot? It shouldn't matter.

"I think she looks great," Masie says, whacking Blaine in the gut. "And you should, too."

Blaine shoots her a dirty look. "I never said she didn't look great. I just think it's weird she's wearing a bikini. I figured that's your influence"—he steps back to eye her up and down—"since that's pretty much all you wear."

Masie smirks then does a little twirl. "I wear it because I look hot. What else should I wear?"

"Clothes." He smirks. "You know, those pieces of fabric that cover up your—"

She swats him again, and he laughs, his eyes crinkling around the corners.

She shakes her head, but a trace of a smile touches her lips. "You're such a perv." Then she whirls around, drops my towel, skips toward the pool, and does a perfect swan dive into the water. When she resurfaces, her hair is dripping wet, water beads her skin, and the water makes her white bikini top kind of see-through. If it was anyone else, I'd tell them. But Masie won't care.

While she's distracted, I pad over to my towel, scoop it up, and wrap it around me.

Blaine, who has had his gaze locked on Masie, finally looks at me again. He frowns when he notices the towel secured around me. "Lex, I didn't mean anything by what I said." He massages the back of his neck. "You just took me by surprise. That's all." His eyes stray to Masie again.

Since when has he been so interested in Masie? He's never showed any interest before. I don't think so anyway.

"I was going to put the towel on before you said anything, but Masie stole it," I tell him, puzzlement twisting inside me. "Well, until I threatened to throw her shoes in the pool."

He chuckles, focusing on me again. "You went right for her heart, huh?"

"Of course," I reply, trying to smile, but he keeps looking at her, making me feel weird. "You know how I work. I don't mess around."

He bites back a smile. "So, you're saying you're tough?"

I lift a brow. "Are you challenging my toughness?"

"Not at all." He's on the verge of laughing.

"Fine, you want to see toughness? I'll show you toughness." I reach out and pinch his arm. Hard.

He busts up laughing, hunching over. "Oh my God, that was the daintiest pinch I've ever felt."

I narrow my eyes at him. "Don't ever dare call me dainty—"

The towel is yanked loose from my body.

Masie snickers from behind me. "Gotcha."

And just like that, almost every part of me is exposed again.

Anger bites underneath my skin as I spin around. But I move too quickly and trip over my feet. I lose my balance, teetering toward the water, when I feel an arm slip around my waist and pull me back to a standing position. My heart thunders in my chest as I realize the muscular arm wrapped around my waist belongs to Blaine.

"You okay there, clumsy girl?" Humor dances in Blaine's tone.

"Do not start with that nickname again." I warn, trying not to squirm from his touch.

Masie gives me a knowing smile, probably thinking I'm in Lust Land again. But I'm not. Not really.

"You promised you'd stop calling me that," I tell Blaine. "I'm not even clumsy."

With another chuckle, Blaine dips his lips toward my ear and pulls me closer. "No, I'm pretty sure you *demanded* I stop calling you that. But I never agreed to it, and I never will. You'll always be my clumsy girl. Even this I'm-too-tough-for-everyone version of you."

"Aw, aren't you two adorable?" Masie says. Then she holds up her hand and pretends to take a photo. "Dammit, I really wish I had my camera right now."

I glare at her, while Blaine laughs, holding me for a beat longer before releasing me.

"You know what I think?" he asks, stepping up beside me, his eyes glimmering mischievously.

Shaking my head, I inch away from him and let out a slow breath, forcing myself to stay composed. "With that look in your eyes, I'm sure I don't want to."

A devilish grin spreads across his face as he winks at me then lunges for Masie. She squeals as he picks her up by the waist and tosses her into the pool. Water splashes everywhere, drenching both Blaine and me.

I gasp from the coldness and step back from the edge of the pool.

"Oh no, you don't," Blaine says, coming at me.

"Don't you dare," I warn, pointing a finger at him as I continue to back away. "You know I hate getting in water."

He's still grinning. "Which makes this much more fun."

He steps toward me, and I step back, preparing to fight him. Grinning, he rushes at me. I may be tough, but with him, I don't even stand a chance. Still, I whirl around and run toward the house.

Two steps later, he wraps his arms around my waist. Writhing, I kick and try to wiggle free. My skin is still wet from Masie's splash, and his hands nearly slip off me, but he manages to hold me tightly, carrying me over to the pool and tossing me into the air. A second later, I splash into the water.

I suck at swimming, so it takes me a moment to kick

back to the top. Right before I surface, a body dives into the water beside me. Blaine, I'm sure.

Breaking through the surface, I suck in a huge breath of air. It takes me a couple breaths to get my bearings, and by the time I do, Blaine is popping up through the water beside me.

"That wasn't funny," I tell him as I paddle my arms to stay afloat.

"You're right." He grins cockily. "It was freaking hilarious."

I mimic his cocky grin and splash water into his face. "So was that."

He curses but laughs, wiping his face with his hand.

Before he can pay me back, I blast him with a sassy smirk then swim toward the edge. I don't climb out, mostly because, when Blaine threw Masie into the pool, she had my towel in her hands, so I don't have anything else to cover up with at the moment. And I want to cover up. Badly.

Masie swims up beside me and grips the edge of the pool with a grin on her face. "Holy crap! He's totally flirting with you."

"He so is not. If anything, he's flirting with you." It hurts like a mothereffer to say it, but I manage to keep a neutral expression.

She rolls her eyes. "Like Blaine would ever flirt with me. Please. I'm not even his type. I mean, sure, he's dated a lot of blondes. But, so what? I've seen him check out brunettes and redheads, too." Her eyes pop wide open. "I so didn't mean he checks out other girls all the time. I've just seen him do it occasionally ... when he's drunk ... really, really drunk." She's a babbling mess.

"I'm fine." Wanting this painful conversation to end, I back paddling toward the ladder so I can climb out of the pool. I'll just have to make sure to get into the house quickly, and then I'll get dressed and never, ever wear a bikini again.

When I reach the ladder, I take a deep breath and hoist myself up. Water rivers off my body, and I wrap my arms around myself as I shuffle toward the back door of Masie's house.

Just get inside so you can cover up.

"Hey! Don't you dare drip water all over my floor," Masie shouts after me.

"That's what you get for ruining my towel," I throw back, gripping the doorknob.

"Lex ..." she whines. "Please don't. I just had the floors cleaned."

"Yeah, well, maybe you should've thought about that before you ruined my towel." I turn around, putting on my best fake smile, but it promptly fades.

Blaine has swum up to her and is saying something with his head tipped close to her. Maybe I'm reading too much into it, but the position they're in looks very intimate.

Is something going on with them?

Masie catches my eye and rolls hers, nudging Blaine away. Her lips part, but Blaine grabs ahold of her and swims farther into the pool. Masie screeches like she's upset, but her laughter reveals otherwise.

"Blaine, stop!" she gripes through her laughter.

I turn around and enter her house, not wanting to see the rest of the moment.

I remain in the washroom until I'm not dripping water anymore. Then I go into the guest room to change. I more than happily peel the bikini off and shove it in my bag. As I reach for my clothes, my gaze strays to the mirror, across my reflection, across each and every flaw.

"You're so fucking ugly," Jay says he crouches down in front of me.

Tears sting in my eyes as I try to back away further from him, but my back hits the wall. I close my eyes, unsure why he came in here. It's the girl's bathroom and it's during class. It's why I ran in here to begin with—because I thought I'd have some privacy to lose my shit, where I could cry my eyes out over my parents. It's only been a week since they died and I thought I was okay, but then I just lost it.

I look away from my reflection and shove the thoughts out of my mind. Taking a deep breath, I hurriedly put on a pair of cut-offs, a black tank top, and then tie a plaid shirt around my waist. Once I do, I feel a little bit better and more in control of myself.

I leave my wet hair down and tug on a pair of clunky boots. When I check my reflection in the mirror, I pull a face. I look like a mess. A hot mess. So, yeah, I pretty much look like I always do. But at least I'm not in that stupid bikini anymore.

I comb my fingers through my tangled, wavy hair a couple of times then grab my bag, my car keys, and head back outside. I was supposed to hang around at Masie's then go to a party later tonight with her, even though I don't want to, but I think I'll go home to shower and wash the chlorine out of my hair then meet up with her later. Or not, if I can find a way out of it.

I step outside, putting on my plastic smile, but then my control dissolves as I spot Masie and Blaine making out in the pool.

He has her pressed up against the side, his hands resting on the edge, her head pinned between them. She is gripping his shoulders, pulling him closer as she kisses him.

I want to look away, but my eyes remain fused to them, the sight of them burning my eyes worse than even the sunlight.

Move, Alexis. Move your damn feet and walk away. Do not react to this. Do not let that mask go down.

I start to turn to go back into the house, but I end up tripping over my own feet. I manage to catch my balance, but not before accidentally kicking a flowerpot off the back porch and onto the barbeque grill below.

"Oh shit." Masie lets out a string of panicked curses. "Lex, wait."

I don't even look at her as I rush into the house and barrel for the front door. Then I charge outside and climb into my car, a beat up 1969 Chevelle, but the engine refuses to turn over.

"Shit. Shit. Shit." I pound my hands against the steering wheel, totally pissed off.

I'm about to pull out my phone to call one of my siblings and see if they'll come get me, when Masie bursts out the front door.

"Lex!" she shouts. She has a towel wrapped around her, panic flooding her expression. "Please just wait a second. I can explain."

For a brief second, I consider running up and kicking her ass. But since I'm still in a little bit of trouble for the last fight I got into, I hop out of my car and run down the driveway. I keep running and running without looking back, wishing I never had to look back again. Wishing I could forget it all—Masie, Blaine, my friendships with them both. My parents' deaths.

I want to forget everything.

Unfortunately, though, that's not a possibility, so I'm left trying to outrun everything. The problem is, it feels like I'm being followed. And I'm not speaking metaphorically.

I peer over my shoulder, half expecting to see Masie right on my tail, but nope. Nothing is there. But I still can't shake the feeling that I'm not completely alone.

2

ALEXIS

Instead of running on the side of the road where Masie and Blaine can find me, I take a shortcut through the park in the middle of the countless cul-de-sacs enclosing Masie's neighborhood, the entire time feeling as if I'm being followed.

When I reach the playground, I flick a glance over my shoulder and my heart bottoms to my stomach when I spot Blaine's truck down the road. *Shit*. He's the last person I want to see right now. Well, and Masie.

Picking up my pace, I sprint toward the playground then duck into the top of a plastic tunnel that leads to a series of slides. Out of breath, because I'm apparently completely out of shape, I peer out of one of the oval, plastic windows and at the road.

Blaine's truck is creeping down the street. I worry he

spotted me, but then he drives past the park and down the street.

Releasing an exhale, I sit down and prop my feet on the wall in front of me. I sit in silence, alone, trying to figure out what the hell is wrong with my car so I can get the hell away from here without worrying about running into Masie or Blaine.

I dig out my phone to do some research on what could be wrong with it then frown at the seventeen missed texts displayed on my screen. Ever since I ran away from Masie's, my phone has been buzzing in my pocket like a crazy lunatic. Most of the texts are from her and a few are from Blaine. My twin sister, Zhara, has also texted me, which is weird. We barely talk anymore, not since our parents died and I decided to leave my good, sweet girl persona behind while she latched on to hers.

Zhara: Call me ASAP, please! I need to talk to you about something super important!

More than likely, she wants to talk about my behavior and how I need to change into a better person. It's a conversation we've had a lot. I can't deal with that right now, though.

I decide to text her a bit later, after I've calmed down. Then I move on to check the rest of my texts. I have one from Loki, my older brother who got guardianship of our brother and sisters after our parents passed away.

Loki: Are you coming home tonight?

Such a simple text, but to me, it says so much more.

Like, how he's tired of me coming home late. Tired of me in general. I don't blame him. I'm a tiring person. And deep down, underneath my I-don't-give-a-shit-about-anything façade, I feel bad. I'm just a mess right now.

I send Loki a quick text back.

Me: Probably to take a shower, but then I'm leaving again.

He doesn't respond, his silence showing how agitated he is with me. Still, I can tell I annoy him whenever I disappear and don't tell him where I'm going, or when I refuse to set plans, or whenever I get fired from a job. I know I need to decide about where I'm going with my life since I'll be graduating in just over a year, but the truth I have no clue what I want to do. I used to love art. I used to love painting. I used to love creating. But none of that matters to me anymore. At least in the way it did before.

I see who the rest of the texts are from. Strangely, I have one from West, Blaine's best friend and my archnemesis since grade school. Sure, the two of us hang out a ton, but only when we're both with Blaine, because we clash big time. The main reason we butt heads is West knows how to push my buttons, and I know I do the same to him. He constantly teases me, and I do the same to him. But at least we both keep the douchiness even.

Things had gotten so bad that Masie and Blaine made up a rule that we aren't allowed to stay in the same room together alone, like they think we're going to beat the crap out of each other. West thought it was funny when they made that rule and joked that they were probably worried we were going to screw each other's brains out. I was unamused. Well, sort of. Fine, I kind of laughed, but only at the idea of having sex with West.

Sure, he's hot, in a blond, Gothic prince sort of way, with his chin-length, blond hair; pierced tongue; and studded, dark clothing. But Blaine is more my type, which is weird because, looking at us, you'd think West and I went together. Not that any guy would want me,

"Dammit," I grit out as my heart begins to pound in my chest.

I don't even know why I'm upset. Blaine is just a guy. A guy I didn't even really want to have a crush on.

But he used to be my friend. So did Masie.

Releasing a shaky exhale, I lift my head and return to my texts, my brows dipping when I see I have one from an unknown number.

My confusion only doubles when I open it.

Unknown: Hi there.

I lift a brow. *What the hell?* It's got to be from a wrong number, right? Yeah, it has to be.

Deciding to ignore it, I tap the internet tab and start searching for what could be wrong with my car. After browsing for a bit, I have a couple of ideas. Not that it's going to help me since, if I want to fix my car, I'm going to have to go back to Masie's house.

"I'm acting like such a coward," I mutter. "I don't like

feeling this way ... I'm usually tougher than this ... God, today sucks balls."

"Hey! My mom says balls is a bad word." A little kid pops his head around the corner and scowls at me. He has what I'm hoping is chocolate all over his face and leaves in his hair. "I'm going to tell."

"I meant balls as in tennis balls," I tell him. "And I don't really care if you tell."

"Well, you will," he says, throwing a twig at me. "And you shouldn't even be in here. You're too old."

"You're never too old to play on a playground. Now go away and leave me alone."

He throws another twig at me, and it pegs me in the eye.

My hand flies to my face. My eye burns like hell. "You little sh—"

He cuts me off with a wicked laugh then bails down the slide.

I pull out my phone to use the camera to try to see the damage. Great. Now I look like I have pink eye. And on top of that, the unknown number didn't take my silence as a hint.

Unknown: What? No response?

Beyond annoyed, I send a quick reply back.

Me: Wrong number, so stop texting me.

I put my phone away and sit on the slide with my hand pressed to my eye until I hear the boy heading back up. He's chattering to someone about a crazy girl who lives in the tunnels. Clearly, it's time to say *peace out* to my hideout.

I glance out the window to make sure Blaine's truck isn't in the parking lot or on the street. Then I climb out of my hiding spot and hike across the grass toward the road. By now, the sky has started to grey as the sun descends behind the shallow hills surrounding Fareland, which means I'm running out of time to fix my car before the sun goes down completely.

Part of me wonders if I should just sneak back to Masie's. Maybe she won't be there. Before I can make up my damn mind, though, a dark blue, 1968 GTO rolls up to the curb in front of me.

My frown deepens.

I know the owner.

Very well.

Too well.

West.

Great. Just what I need. Here I am, close to having a breakdown, and my worst enemy is here to witness it.

Yeah, today definitely sucks balls.

3

WEST

I've been helping Blaine and Masie look for Alexis for the past hour after Masie called me, hysterical, sobbing so hard I could barely understand her. To be honest, I almost hung up on her. Not because I'm a dick—okay, well, sometimes I can be—but I've never been a fan of Masie's, at least not enough to deal with her drama. That's always been Blaine's thing. Ever since the beginning of high school when Alexis introduced us to her, Blaine's had a thing for Masie. And Alexis has had a thing for Blaine.

It's a whole drama-filled love triangle that no one thankfully talks about. Honestly, I don't think Blaine realizes it exists. I have no idea how he doesn't. If he paid attention for two seconds, he'd be able to tell Alexis has been in love with him since the beginning of high school. But while Blaine's been my friend, he's always been a self-centered dumbass.

He sees what he wants to see, and a lot of what he sees is himself.

How Alexis can be in love him is beyond me. Even I can barely tolerate him sometimes, and I'm supposed to be his best friend. Then again, we haven't really been best friends since he made the varsity football team and started thinking he was the shit while I focused on my grades, but that was mainly because my parents forced me to.

"You'll get straight A's every year," my dad had told me at the start of high school. "Or else there will be consequences."

He didn't have to state what the consequences were. I knew the drill by that point. Had scars on my body to remind me.

"Go away," Alexis snaps at me, tearing me away from my thoughts. "You're the last person I want to see right now."

"Well, hello to you, too," I quip as I pull my car up beside her.

In reality, her comment stings. Why? Well, how do I explain this in a way that won't make me sound like a love-struck dumbass? Hmm ... Okay, here it goes ...

I, West, am in love with Alexis.

Yeah, I know I sound like a total love-struck dumbass.

Love-struck dumbasses aside, it's the truth. Our little friendship love triangle is actually a square; has been since a certain night a couple of years ago when Alexis and I stayed up playing cards and drinking whiskey, and I poured my heart and soul out to her—drunkenly, of course.

I told her how my parents' constant fighting was messing with my head, although I left out the part about how they were fighting with me, too. I've never told anyone about the stuff that goes on in my house behind closed doors.

Alexis didn't laugh at me when I confided in her, which sort of surprised me. Before then, we'd always latched on to the opportunity to make fun of one another. But this time she didn't. She hugged me and told me everything was going to be okay.

"I promise it'll get better," she assures me.

"How do you know that?" My voice cracks. "Maybe it won't. Honestly, it never does."

"Because you're you," she says, pulling me closer. "I'd probably never admit this while sober, but you're, like, the strongest person I know. Well, besides me. But I'm a freakin' anomaly."

I chuckle, but on the inside, I'm wound up tight.

God, she had smelled so good that night. Like whiskey and cotton candy. I wanted to take a bite. The thought had startled me at the time, but not enough to stop me from getting hard. But seriously? Since when had Alexis turned me on? We'd been frenemies forever, and I'd never thought of her that way before. Okay, maybe I had a couple of times.

Alexis is gorgeous, even though she doesn't realize it. She doesn't show off her sexiness either, like Masie or some of the other girls in our school. And she's smart, which is always a bonus. And she always seems more interested in books than hooking up.

But anyway, back at the time, I hadn't admitted all of that to myself. But as she hugged me and told me everything was going to be okay, all I could think was: *Damn, she smells so good, and she's so damn warm.* Plus, it had been a long time since someone had hugged me. I found myself wanting to kiss her, and I probably would've, too, if Blaine hadn't woken up from being passed out on the floor and puked all over the carpet.

Yep, if that won't kill the mood, I don't know what will.

It didn't really matter anyway. That vomit probably saved me from making an ass out of myself.

After the moment Alexis and I shared, I was a goner, even if I didn't realize it at the time. And no, I didn't fall in love with her then. It took some time, a year at least of hanging out with her and trying not to ask if she wanted to reenact my favorite porn scenes.

It wasn't just about that, though. The truth is, underneath her rough exterior, Alexis is kind, caring, and fun. Sure, she constantly teases me, but only because I give her shit all the time. Honestly, I think it's our way of flirting, even if she'll never admit it. And I love getting her to smile. And she deserves to smile, all the damn time. But after her parents died, those smiles became less and less frequent. If I could, I'd try to make her smile all the time.

Since she's never given any sign of reciprocating my

feelings, I've kept how I feel locked away. I'm good at that—locking shit away where no one can find it. I'm good at pretending things are always okay. Just like I'm fantastic at pretending I haven't been in love with Lex for a while.

Yeah, I know. I'm pathetic. But I can't help how I feel, just like Lex can't help how she feels, just like Blaine can't help how his dick feels, and Masie can't help how she needs to be the center of attention twenty-four seven.

Yeah, feelings suck. They really do. And sometimes I think I'd be better off without them. But, so far, I haven't been able to figure out how to make that happen, which is why I'm still here with Lex, even after she tells me to get lost.

I park at the curb and push the shifter into park.

"Now, is that any way to talk to your friend?" I tease, sneaking in a moment to discreetly check her out, unsure of what she'd do if she actually caught me, but I don't really care at the moment.

Her hair is a tangled mess of brown waves that flow down her back; she doesn't have a drop of makeup on; and her shorts show off her long, lean legs.

Yep, there goes the mental porn show again.

"Your very best friend, for that matter," I add.

She rolls her eyes. "You're not my best friend. And really, I doubt you think that."

I press my hand to my chest. "Wow, that really hurts. After all these years, I thought we were like this." I hold up my hand with my fingers crossed. "Now, come to find out, I've been living a delusional lie."

"A lie you've been telling yourself," she quips. "I had nothing to do with it."

"Yeah, right, you've totally been sending mixed signals."

She narrows her gaze at me, yet a playful glint flickers in her eyes. "I so have not."

"You have, too." I fake pout. "Think about all those times we shared secrets, painted each other's toenails, and braided each other's hair."

She rolls her eyes again. "Hate to break it to ya, but you and Blaine have been doing the BFF thing all wrong. That's not what best friends do."

"Well, don't tell him that." I wink. "I like getting my hair braided."

She eyeballs my chin-length, blond hair and smirks. "I bet you do. And I bet you look really pretty, too."

"Aw, you think I'm pretty?"

"Pretty annoying."

"Ouch, Lex, you're aiming straight for my heart today."

Her gaze drops to the ground, and I get the feeling she's trying to hide the hurt flooding her eyes. "Yeah, well, I'm in a shitty mood," she mumbles, kicking at the dirt with the tip of her boot. "Sorry. I shouldn't take it out on you."

"It's okay. I get it." I pause, unsure of what the right thing to say is, or if there's even a right thing to say. "Masie called me about an hour ago."

Her gaze snaps up to mine, her eyes so big and gorgeous yet conveying so much pain that it makes me want to punch Blaine and burn all of Masie's clothes because, to her, that's about the equivalent of a kick to the balls.

She eyes me over warily. "What exactly did she tell you?"

"That you caught her and Blaine kissing in the pool."

"Oh." She grows silent, her expression guarded. "Aren't you wondering why that'd upset me?"

I hesitate. "I already know ... Have for a while now."

Her expression plummets, and she starts to step back like she's going to run away.

"Oh no, you don't." I hop out of the car and reach to grab ahold of her, but she spins around and takes off toward the playground.

I could just let her go, let her hide away until she feels like talking, but that's not really my style. So, I chase after her, and when I catch up to her, I wrap my arms around her waist and haul her back against me. Her back slams into my chest, and she curses like a sailor. Me, I go completely hard as her ass presses against me.

God, that feels so good ... like, really good. I want to kiss her so damn badly ...

God, this whole love thing is getting completely out of hand.

"Um, West?" she says with a nervous edge in her tone. "You doing okay back there?"

I suddenly realize three things:

1.She's gone still in my arms.

2.I have her pressed so close she can probably feel my hard-on.

3.My lips have wandered to her neck, and I've started to suck on her skin. Like, one-step-away-from-I'm-going-to-suck-your-blood kind of suck.

"Yeah?" I clear my throat a stupid amount of times.

Normally, I'm not such a babbling pussy. I can be quite charming when I want to be, even when I'm feeling like shit. In fact, I'm a pro at covering up what I'm feeling. But, with Alexis, I'm way too aware that my feelings for her will end with my heart ripped out of my chest.

See? Again, point proven—feelings suck.

"Are you sure?" She sounds confused. "Or, have you recently been bitten by a vampire? If you're not sure, we can cross-reference your symptoms with the vampire symptoms list. I'm sure there's something on the internet."

Okay, now she just sounds amused.

My lips part with a snarky comeback, but she interrupts me.

"Stupid, shit, damn, crap, troll babies." She's breathing so heavily you'd think the damn girl just ran a marathon.

"Well, that was attractive," I joke with a smirk.

"I'm not trying to be attractive." She wiggles out of her arms, spins around, and crouches down in front of me, putting her face right by my dick. "Masie's over there in the parking lot."

I glance to my right and, sure enough, Masie is

wandering around the parking lot, glancing inside cars. Still, that doesn't explain …

"Look, I get why you don't want to see her"—I slip my fingers through her hair, fighting the urge to push her closer to my dick—"but I'm really confused about how acting like you're going to suck me off is going to keep her from spotting you. I mean, don't get me wrong, if we were in my car, I'd totally let you suck away. But I don't want our first time to be in front of half the damn neighborhood."

She trips to her feet. The shocked look on her face has me verging toward laughing my ass off, but the flush spreading across her cheeks distracts me.

God, she's so beautiful …

I start to step forward to … well, I'm not sure, but something that'll definitely only get more blood pumping through me. Then I get cock-blocked by a blonde-haired, screaming banshee running across the grass straight at us.

"Lex!" Masie screeches, waving her hands in the air like we can't already see or hear her. Everyone within a five-mile radius probably can.

Alexis gives me a helpless, pleading look. It's a look that would get me to agree to do anything, even eat a strawberry. And no, I'm not kidding, Strawberries are weird with their seeds and their squishiness. They shouldn't even be considered food.

"I don't want to talk to her," Alexis says, her big eyes pleading with me to help her.

I don't think. I just act, grabbing her hand. "Then let's get out of here." I take off toward my car and smile when she follows.

If only she wasn't following me just to run away.

4

ALEXIS

I can't believe I'm running away with West. I can't believe West is helping me. I can't believe I want his help. No, what I really can't believe is that West was getting a little too happy down south while he was holding me.

I almost panicked and ran, and not just because West got a hard-on ...

Honestly, I doubt that was because of me. Maybe he was looking at someone else.

He had to be.

"Where do you want me to take you?" West asks after we hop into his car.

I blink at him. *Huh? What did he just say?*

"Um, what?"

The corner of his lips tugs up into a lopsided smirk. "Jeez, I never knew you had such a dirty mind." He pauses, chewing on his bottom lip. "But, if you really want to, then ..." He gives an insinuating look at the back seat while waggling his eyebrows. "I've always wanted to do it in my back seat."

I roll my eyes. "Yeah right. Like you haven't screwed someone there already. You're such a little manwhore."

His brow arches upward. "Says who?"

"Says everyone."

"When's the last time you heard someone say I'm a manwhore?"

"Um ..." Come to think of it, it's been a while. "I don't know ... Maybe a year or two ago."

"Exactly," he says. "And you know why I was like that back then."

True. A couple of years ago, West admitted his parents were fighting all the time, which was weird to hear since most of the town thought they were the perfect couple. Even West had thought so. When they started fighting all the time, his view on love changed. At least, that's what he told me one night after we raided Blaine's dad's whiskey cabinet. Blaine had passed out after three shots—the dude's such a lightweight—and West and I stayed up playing cards.

I hugged him that night and, for the craziest moment, I thought he was going to kiss me. But he didn't, so I'm pretty sure I misread the entire situation. Wouldn't be the first time. Thankfully, Blaine woke up and puked all over the floor. Yeah, it was gross, but it stopped me from doing something stupid, like leaning in with my lips puckered like a fish. I can only imagine what West would've said if I had. It would've given him plenty of ammunition for jokes. Like enough to last him at least a year or so.

Definitely not one of my finer moments—

I'm yanked from my thoughts as Masie nears the car, shouting meaningless apologies at the top of her lungs.

"West, please get me away from the raving lunatic running right at your car," I say in a desperate plea. "I don't know what I'll do if I talk to her, and honestly, I don't want to deal with it right now."

"Oh, yeah, right," he says, like he forgot all about Masie, which would definitely be a first for a guy. He revs up the engine. "Let's get you out of here." He shifts gears and presses on the gas, the tires spinning and kicking up a cloud of dirt as we peel out of the parking lot.

I peer over my shoulder and out the window, Masie is surrounded by a cloud of dust, her hair messed up, and she's missing one shoe.

Okay, now that's a picture I thought I'd never see.

"You look way too pleased right now," West teases as we speed down the road.

"Sorry." But I'm really not.

"You don't need to be sorry about it. Masie deserves a face full of dirt." He sighs, gripping the steering wheel. "She deserves more for what she did to you."

I pick at my fingernails, feeling squirmy over how much he seems to understand the situation. I hate feeling squirmy.

"How long have you known? I mean, about me ... liking ..." I exhale loudly. "How long have you known I liked Blaine?"

He lifts a shoulder. "I first thought you did when we were about sixteen."

Blood roars in my eardrums. "How? I mean, what gave me away?"

He moves one hand off the steering wheel to reach over and graze his finger along the corner of my eye. "It was the way you looked at him."

"Oh." I frown. "I didn't realize I was that obvious."

"It wasn't that obvious," he assures. "At least, not enough for Blaine to catch on."

I almost relax. "So, he doesn't know?"

He shakes his head, returning his hand to the steering wheel. "He's never said anything to me."

I release a breath of relief. "That's good."

He cocks his brow. "Why?"

"Why the hell would I want him to know I'm in love with him?"

His fingers tense on the steering wheel. "So, you are in love with him, huh?"

Am I?

Maybe Before, but now...

I don't even think I know what love is anymore.

"I thought you already said you knew I was?" I ask, avoiding answering.

He shrugs. "I knew you liked him, and I guessed you

might be in love with him, but I wasn't completely sure." He looks away, focusing on the road, his lean arms tense.

And while I'm not sure what has him so wound up, I seize the opportunity to stare out the window and collect my thoughts.

"Are you sure you are, though?" West asks so suddenly I jump.

I glance at him. "Am I sure what?"

"That you're in love with him?"

"What kind of question is that?" I sound offended, and I don't even know why. He didn't do anything to me. None of this is his fault.

"I didn't mean to piss you off." He gives me an apologetic, sidelong glance. "But sometimes people think they're in love with someone, when their feelings are more of an infatuation than actual love."

"You say that like you're speaking from experience."

"Nah. It takes me a lot to fall in love with someone."

"Have you ever been in love before?" I reach into my pocket to silence my phone as it buzzes again. My fingers brush across my car keys, reminding me of another problem I have to deal with—my car broken down in Masie's driveway.

Crap.

His jaw clenches as he stares ahead at the road. "Maybe once or twice."

"Did someone break your heart?"

"I'm not sure yet."

I angle my head to the side in confusion. "That doesn't really make any sense."

"Of course it does." He catches my gaze. "If I haven't told the person I'm in love with them."

My lips for an O. "Okay, I get it. So, we're kind of in the same boat then, since I haven't told Blaine how I feel either."

"Maybe." He restlessly taps his fingers on top of the steering wheel. "Do you think you will?"

I shake my head. "Definitely not now."

"Do you think you would've if"—he hesitates—"if you hadn't caught Masie and Blaine doing ... well, you know?"

No, I don't know what he means. Sure, I saw them kissing, but that doesn't mean it was the first time they made out. For all I know, they've hooked up a ton and I've just been blind and naïve. Then, why did Masie keep insisting Blaine likes me and encouraging me to go for it? Who knows? Perhaps she was messing with my head and getting some sort of twisted pleasure out of watching my heart shatter. That doesn't really sound like Masie, but at this point, I'm not sure I know her at all. Maybe I never did. Perhaps she was one of those plastic people—fake on the outside and the inside.

What I do know is that I wouldn't have told Blaine. Not when I'm certain he wouldn't feel the same way. Not when it means I'd have to deal with heartbreak, with emotions and feelings and all that shit I work so hard to fight back.

"No, I wouldn't've told him," I say with a shrug.

He nods, silence stretching between.

"What is that in your hand?" he asks suddenly, his gaze dropping to my hand.

"What? This?" I hold up my car keys. "My car broke down at Masie's."

"That sucks." He pauses, considering something. "Maybe I can help you fix it. You know I'm good at that stuff."

"I know, but I don't like freebies."

"Maybe it could be a belated birthday present," he suggests, glancing at me.

"You already gave me a present," I remind him, looking down at the studded leather band I am currently wearing on my wrist.

We may fight like angry cats most of the time, but he always gives me the best gifts.

He glances down at the bracelet as well and a small smile pulls at his lips before he returns his attention to the road. "I don't mind helping you out. It's not a freebie or anything. It's just one friend helping another."

"We're friends?" I ask, partially teasing, but partially serious.

He lifts a shoulder. "I think so. It kind of hurts that you don't."

I feel kind of bad in that moment, which is weird. Maybe that's why I briefly lose my sanity and say, "All right, you can help me if you want." I sit up straighter in the seat. "But I want to do most of the work."

He chuckles. "Okay, cute girl."

"Okay ..." I trail off. Wait. Back the hell up. "Did you just call me cute?"

He smiles. "I've called you cute before."

I roll my eyes. "Yeah, when you were teasing me which, FYI, you do all the time."

"How do you know I'm teasing you when I do it?" He smiles, highly amused. "Maybe I mean everything I've ever said to you."

"So, you really believe I'm a fairy princess from the realm of Spoiled Brat?" I repeat the nickname he gave me in fifth grade.

"Hey, that was a long time ago. You can't hold that against me, or I'll hold it against you that you called me West the pest who lives in a rat's nest." His muses over something. "You know, when I really think about it, we were pretty clever for grade schoolers."

"*I* may have been clever," I tease. "You were just cleverly stupid."

Narrowing his eyes, he reaches over and lightly pinches me on the thigh in a ticklish sort of way.

I nearly jump out of my seat. I hate being tickled, and West knows that. Yet, he repeats the movement.

"Take that back, Alexis with the pretty blue eyes."

"Never!" My eyes water as he continues to tickle me, laughter bursting from my lips—

I'm thrown forward, my seatbelt locking up and throwing me right back against the seat.

When I blink at the front of the car, Masie is standing there with her hands out in front of her, eyes huge, breathing fiercely, her face bright red.

"What the hell is that crazy woman doing?" West mumbles as he shoves the shifter into park. Then he sticks his head out the window and yells, "Do you have a death wish or something?"

"Oh, shut the hell up!" she snaps at him before she skates her gaze back to mine. She swallows hard, her eyes watering. "Lex, please, just listen to me, okay?" She positions herself in front of the car, putting her hands on the hood and raising her voice over the grumbling engine. "I didn't mean for it to happen ... We were just swimming, and he kissed me." She shakes her head. "But that's no excuse. I'm your best friend, and I should've talked to you first before I did anything."

For a brief moment, I feel kind of bad for her. She looks so tormented, so upset ...

Wait ... I rewind over what she just said.

"Are you saying you *wanted* to kiss Blaine?" I snap. "That you've thought about it before?"

More tears pool in her eyes, her bottom lip quivering as she fights not to cry. "I didn't mean to fall for him. It just sort of happened."

I ball my hands into fights and stab my fingernails into my flesh until I feel the skin break apart.

"For how long?" I ask in an eerily calm voice.

A crease forms at her brows. "What do you mean?"

"How long have you two been hooking up?" Yes, it's an assumption, but I know Masie well. When she wants a guy, she doesn't mess around; she just goes for it. So, if she's saying she likes Blaine, then ...

I swallow the lump crammed in my throat. Her silence says it all.

"So, it's true, then?" My tone sounds so hollow as I shove every ounce of pain I have deep down inside me. "That wasn't the first time you guys kissed?"

Tears spill from her eyes as she slowly shakes her head. "We've been seeing each other for a few months. I'm so sorry. I wanted to tell you, but I—"

"You *wanted* to tell me?" I shake my head. "Sure you did."

"I did," she insists. "I swear, I did."

"Sure, whatever. That's why you continued to encourage me to go for it with him. Why would you do that if you knew my heart was just going to get broken?"

She's crying so hard now, snot running down her face. "I'm so sorry. I thought, if I kept pretending like nothing was happening between Blaine and me, you wouldn't find out." She sobs. "But things got so out of hand ... And Blaine, he kept saying we should tell you so this wouldn't happen. But I was so scared."

I curl my hands into tighter fists. "You *told* Blaine I like him?"

Her bottom lip starts to quiver. "I'm sorry. It just sort of slipped out. He was flirting with me, and I said I couldn't date him. He kept pushing me, asking why, and I let it slip." She rushes toward the passenger side of the car and grips the door. "Please, don't let this ruin our friendship. I know we can get past this." Her gaze flicks to West then back to me. "Just come someplace with me. Someplace where we can talk. Just you and me. I know we can fix this. Please, please, please." She's babbling hysterically.

And I feel nothing.

The friendship we had is gone, withering away like the flowers on my parents' graves.

I look at West. "Just go before I get out and kick her ass."

Nodding, he reaches for the shifter while Masie lets out a heart-wrenching sob.

"Lex, no, no, no," she babbles, trying to open my door. "We can't just let this go. We need to fix this. You're my best friend!"

I shake my head, lock the door, and start to roll up the window. "No, we're not. In fact, I'm not sure we ever were." The words cut against my lips, carrying so much truth.

I may have thought Masie and I were best friends, but that wasn't real. Best friends don't do what she did to me. And the friendship we once had will never be the same.

Not ever again.

5

ALEXIS

After West drives away, leaving Masie in another cloud of dust and a sea of self-pitying tears, I remain quiet for a long time. So long that I'm sure I start to freak him out. But I can't find any words to follow what just went down. How can I when I'm not even certain how I feel?

Feelings. What I would give for them to go away. I've tried too hard to make that happen and have succeeded for months, but now everything is going to crap.

"Oh my God, feelings suck," I mutter, pinching the brim of my nose.

West lets out a hollow laugh.

I shoot him a perplexed look, and he holds up a hand in front of him.

"Sorry," he says. "It's just that ... I think that same thing all the time."

"That feelings suck?"

"Yep."

"Is that why you haven't ever been in a real relationship? Or is that because of your parents?" Shaking my head, I look away. What am I doing? Prying into his life like this, getting to know him? "You know what? Forget I said that. It's none of my business."

"No, it's fine ... And the answer is neither."

I flit a glance in his direction. "Really?"

He nods, biting back a smile. "Yes, really."

"Why do you seem so smiley about that?"

He lifts a shoulder. "You should know by now that I'm a smiley sort of guy."

I snort a laugh but hastily bite down on my tongue to stifle the noise. "Sure, you are."

He presses his hand to his chest. "How you wound me so?"

I roll my eyes. "Easy, wannabe Shakespeare."

"You know, normal girls like that romantic shit."

"Well, I'm not a normal girl."

"No, you're not."

The way he says it confuses me. But not as much as the way he's looking at me.

"Why are you looking at me like that?" I ask.

"Like what?" He keeps looking at me in the same way.

I eye him over. "I don't know ... like you're a sugar junkie, and I'm a candy bar."

He sinks his teeth into his lip and turns away, staring at

the road and gripping the wheel so tightly that his knuckles turn white. "You have no idea," he mutters. "No damn idea."

"Okay, what the hell is that supposed to mean?"

Instead of answering, he shrugs, keeping his focus on the road, acting weird, even for him.

I eyeball him over, wondering what the hell he's thinking right now. And not knowing makes me feel squirmy and uneasy.

"Okay, now why are *you* looking at me like that?" he asks, releasing his lip from his teeth.

"I'm not looking at you in any way." I yank my attention off him then change the subject. "So, where are we going?"

It takes him a moment to say anything, his gaze boring a hole into the side of my head. I feel like I'm going to crawl out of my scarred skin.

"I'll let you off the hook for now. Next time you look at me like that though, I'm going to get the truth out of you." His tone turns devious. "No matter what it takes."

"Oh no, not the *no matter what it takes* threat," I mock with an eye roll.

A small smile touches West's lips as he drives down the road, but then he frowns. "We're going to Masie's," he says as he glances at his phone.

"What!" My attention snaps to him. "No. Don't take me back there. I'm worried if I see her again, I'll kick her ass. And I can't get arrested again."

"Again, huh?" He glances at me. "What's your number up to now?"

"I don't know ... like, five, maybe."

"You're lucky your sister has a cop for a friend."

"Yeah, probably."

He grins, and the corners of my lips quirk up into an almost smile, yet I don't quite make it there.

He sighs. "Look, I think we need to go to Masie's so we can look at your car and see if we need to pick up any parts."

I guess he's right, but still ...

"Do we have to do that tonight?" I ask. "I'd kind of like a break from her, at least for the rest of the night."

"Okay ... But eventually you're going to have to get it over with."

"I know but ... can we, like, do it tomorrow?"

He hesitates. "Sure."

He seems so squirrely suddenly ...

"What aren't you telling me?" I ask.

"Nothing," he says with a shrug.

"West, just tell me. You've always been honest with me, even when the truth hurts."

"That's not completely true. Remember that one time when I saw your cat get ran over and I didn't tell you for a week because I knew you'd get upset?"

"Oh yeah, I forgot about that." I drum my fingers on top of my knee. "I actually thought that was kind of nice of you, though." Back when I actually thought I deserved nice.

He crooks a brow. "Really? Because you seemed pissed off at the time."

I sigh. "Yeah, I know. And I'm sorry I was. I just get that way sometimes. Besides, I think part of why I reacted that way is because there's always sort of been this challenge thing going on between us."

"What do you mean?" he asks too innocently.

I give him an unimpressed look. "I think you know what I mean."

"Okay, maybe I do."

"Then why pretend you don't?"

He shrugs. "Because I don't want it to exist anymore." He shrugs again, seeming confused and kind of vulnerable. "When I first met you, it was pretty clear you weren't a fan of mine, so I played it off by teasing you."

Really? That's what this little thing between us has been about?

"It's not that I didn't not like you. You just know how to push my buttons."

His brow curves upward. "Really? Because sometimes it seems like you hate me."

I blow out a breath, unsure of what to say to that. "Look, I know we tease each other and everything, but I've never thought: *Hey, I hate West.* In fact, I've always thought you were kind of funny, even when I'm the butt of your jokes."

"You've never been the butt of my jokes. And I'm sorry if I made you feel that way." He nibbles on his lip undecidedly. I can tell the moment he arrives at a decision, because he smirks. "I've always thought of our little bantering as flirting."

"Yeah right."

He gives me a dubious look. "Deep down, I know you think the same thing."

I glare at him. "I so do not."

He smirks. "Sure, you don't."

"I do not and stop saying that."

"What? Stop saying the truth? That just seems silly." A wicked glint flickers in his eyes. "Besides, back at the park, I could tell you liked me biting your neck."

"No, I didn't." And it's not a total lie. Not that I hated it ... I just ... "Dude, you're about to get your ass kicked."

He grins. "Aw, please don't tease me."

"I'm not joking."

"Whatever you say."

His indifference drags the fire out of me, something I haven't felt in a long time.

"The neck biting thing was the most unpleasant experience I've ever had," I say. "And I'm going to show you." I lean over, put my mouth beside his neck, part my lips, and then sink my teeth into him. I don't bite hard enough to draw blood, but he's definitely going to have some teeth marks on his skin. Then I move back and smirk. "See?"

He doesn't respond, just pulls the car over and turns off the engine.

"What're you ...?" I trail off as he leans over and puts his mouth on my neck, gently grazing his teeth along my skin as he sucks and nips and bites. I can feel the cold metal of his tongue ring against my skin, and I gasp, clutching on to him, goosebumps sprouting across my flesh ...

I jerk back, panting, my mind racing so swiftly that I can barely process where I am and I can barely get air into my lungs as painful memories sear at my brain.

West whispers something incoherent before he pulls away with his lips pressed together. "Sorry," he mumbles, seeming unsure of himself and unlike the West I know.

I let out a shaky exhale. "It's fine. I just ... I'm so confused ... I just don't understand why you did that. I mean, it's not like you're attracted to me. And we aren't ... I mean ..." I trail off, realizing I'm rambling.

A strange look crosses West's face and, for a moment, I worry he can see behind my mask. But then he says, "You do realize me and almost every guy that goes to our school thinks you're hot, right?"

I shake my head. "That's not true, and I know it isn't."

He frowns. "Lex, whatever happened freshman and sophomore year with those guys, they were just dumbasses who wanted to mess with your head for blowing them off. The shit they said wasn't true."

I look away, hearing Jay and his friends' words echoing in my head and feeling the stuff they did to me. Feeling the day Jay touched me without my permission.

Of course West can say what he's saying. All he knows

about what happened is from the little Masie once told him and Blaine, despite my protests. And that was basically that Jay and his friends were being jerks to me, which is all anyone really knows. No one needs knows about how much they teased me, the cornering in the hallways, the shit they wrote on my locker, that frightening moment on that bathroom floor...

"Lex, look at me," West says in the softest tone, and I almost do. But then his phone rings, and he answers it with a grumbled, "Hello?"

When he doesn't say anything else, I glance at him and find his eyes fixed on me.

"Yeah ... No, she's here with me." He gives a short pause. "Yeah, I'm pretty sure she doesn't want to talk to you, man." Another pause. "No, I'm not going to tell you where we are." He grows quiet, shaking his head, then snaps, "Look, if she wants to talk to you, she'll call you, okay? I gotta go." Then he hangs up.

The reality of the day sweeps over me again. "Let me guess; that was Blaine?"

He nods, uneasiness flooding his expression. "He wanted to talk to you."

"Oh." I press my lips together.

The idea of talking to Blaine ever again makes me want to break something. And what's even worse is I know I'm eventually going to have to, even if I don't want to. Fareland is a really small town. Plus, we go to school together.

"I figured you wouldn't want to talk to him, but"—

West searches my eyes and a crinkle forms between his brows—"maybe I'm wrong." His lips sink into a frown. "If you do, you can call him. I'm sure he'd love that." A drop of bitterness creeps into his tone, and he quickly clears his throat.

I assess him closely. "Are you okay?"

He dismisses me with a smile. "I'm always okay."

"West," I start, but he drives forward. "Where are we going?"

"I'm taking you home," he tells me. "Then, tomorrow, if you still want to, I'll pick you up and help you fix your car."

"Okay, that sounds good."

Ten minutes later, West is pulling into my driveway. I unbuckle my seatbelt and climb out without uttering a word, ready to get the hell away from this awkward car ride. Well, most of it has been awkward. Not all of it, though. Honestly, West made me feel sort of better, which is weird to think about.

"Lex," West calls out as I'm about to shut the door.

I pause then lower my head and glance into the cab. "Yeah?"

He rests his arm on the console as he leans over it. "Can we ...? Can we just forget that neck kissing thing happened?"

Relief trickles through me. "Yeah, definitely."

He smiles in relief, but then hesitancy crosses his expression. "Do you ... think we can try to be friends?"

I almost say no, partly because of the whole neck kissing thing and partly because this is West and ... well, it's tough picturing us as friends. Plus, I'm really starting to suck at this whole friend thing. I had two left in this world and now they're gone.

But I find myself nodding despite my mind's protests and warnings. "Yeah, okay. I guess we could try."

"Okay, cool." He moves to sit back in his seat. "I'll text you tomorrow when I'm ready to go work on your car. Hopefully, we can get it fixed in one day."

"Thanks." I shut the door and head into my house.

When I step inside, I slump back against the door, the painful emotions of today trying to surface again.

I'm not going to lose it here.

I push away from the door and head for my room. But then decide to do something else, something that'll make me feel better. I spin around and slip back out the front door. Then I go out to the garage to grab my backpack filled with spray paint. I used to love to stain canvases with my soul, but I haven't done that since my parents died. I have, however, found another alternative to express myself. One that I could get in trouble for if I got caught.

Once I get my supplies, I leave the garage and hike down the sidewalk, heading toward the central part of town. Since I live in a subdivision that's located a few miles out of town, it takes me a while to get to the area where most of the stores and shops are. By the time I arrive, I'm hot and getting sweaty, but I don't care. All I care about is doing this and getting it all out of me.

I veer down the nearest alley. Then I drop my bag to the ground, take out a can of spray paint, and glance around to make sure no one is watching. Once I'm satisfied that I'm alone, I lift the can to the wall, which is the side of a store, and paint the bricks with my pain.

Today, she learned the definition of betrayal.
A thorn got lodged in her heart,
But her heart was already woven with thorns
So really, did the betrayal matter?
Maybe one day she'll find out.
But maybe she won't.
Not everything has an answer.
— Signed with a Kiss

I always sign it the same way, but everything I spray onto the walls is different and are in random places across town. It's really starting to annoy the townspeople, and the police are offering a reward for anyone who can bring in the person behind it. That should scare me enough to stop, but I can't seem to make myself care.

As I stand in the alley, looking up at the art I created that now stains this building, I feel my control coming back. I lower my head and my hands against the bricks hard enough that my palms split open.

Air in.

Air out.

Just breathe.

And that's what I do. I keep breathing until every last ounce of pain leaves me and dissolves into the paint-saturated air. Then I walk away, feeling kind of better,

But then I spot him.

Jay and his friends, standing in the parking lot next door and passing around what looks a bottle of tequila. His face looks a bit sunburned, but other than that he looks put together. Nice clothes, styled brown hair, straight white teeth that glisten against the sunlight when he smiles. But it's all a façade. A mask that covers up darkness.

"Yeah, you should definitely screw her," Jay says as he hands one of his friends the bottle. "I did a few months ago. She's a pretty good lay. Well, when she's out of it. When she's sober, she talks too much—"

I whirl around and walk off in the other direction. My heart is racing inside my chest and my skin is crawling.

I'm about to lose it.

But then phone buzzes from inside my pocket, distracting me. I dig it out of my pocket and read the message. Then I instantly frown as I see who the text is from.

Masie: Oh my God! I know you're mad at Blaine and me right now, but seriously, I didn't think you'd do something this bad.

What in the heck is she talking about?

Me: I've done a lot of bad things, so you're gonna have to be more specific.

Masie: You had West punch Blaine! His face is so swollen! And he's really upset about it!

West punched Blaine? Why ...? Huh ...? What?

Me: Hate to break it to you, but I didn't tell West to do that. Guess you're gonna have to find another way to try to guilt-trip me into forgiving you.

Masie: This is so ridiculous. Why can't you just talk to me? Blaine wants to talk to you, too. Please, just talk to us.

I shake my head. While I don't want to talk to Masie, I have even less desire to talk to Blaine. Just the idea of seeing him again ... now that I know he's aware that I feel that way about him ...

Dammit. I'm going to have to see him at school next week. I don't want to.

Another messages pings through and I move to read it, assuming it's Masie. But it's not.

Unknown: Nope, I know I don't have the wrong number, Alexis. I know who I'm texting, just like you know Blaine will never love you.

Confusion and panic spin through me.

Me: Then who the hell is this?

They don't answer right away and, for some reason, I feel like I'm being messed with.

Or maybe the text message *is* from Masie. I mean, before today, I wouldn't have thought she'd do something like this, but now ...

Crap, this is bad. I need to figure out who it is and fast. I'm just not sure how yet.

6

WEST

It's bugging the hell out of me as I drive away from Alexis's house—that sad, hurt look in her eyes ... I can't stand it. While I know I won't be able to take her pain away, there is one thing I can do. Will it get me in trouble? Yep, probably. And if my dad finds out, he'll beat my ass. But I'm used to that sort of crap—the anger my dad directs toward me. Deep down, I know he hates me. And I used to wonder why, why he hated me so much. But honestly, I don't care anymore.

I drive straight from Alexis's to Blaine's house. His truck is in the driveway, so I know he's here. I send him a text before I hop out.

Me: Meet me outside.

As I'm hiking up the driveway, the front door is opened and Blaine walks out. I keep my cool pretty well until Masie steps out behind him.

61

Mascara is smeared all over her face, and her eyes are swollen. Clearly, she's been crying, but I don't care. Masie is a stuck-up snob and a terrible friend to Alexis. She's always trying to change her and is constantly pointing out her flaws. And now she's hooked up with Blaine. Not that I'm surprised. They're both perfect for each other. Plus, Masie always gets what she wants no matter who gets hurt. Trust me, I know firsthand about the damage Masie can do just to get what she wants.

"You're seriously with her right now?" I ask Blaine as I start up the porch.

Blaine's forehead creases as he glances from Masie to me. "Yeah ... Why do you sound so upset about it?"

I roll my tongue in my mouth, biting back my irritation. "Do you even care that you hurt Lex today?"

"Why do you care about this so much?" Blaine asks with an arch of his brow.

"Because Lex and I are friends."

"Since when?"

I inch toward him, the boards creaking under my boots. "She's just as much my friend as she is yours. Honestly, after this, she's probably not your friend anymore."

His expression falters. "Look, I don't know what she told you, but I didn't lead her on or anything. I've always made it clear I just want to be friends with her." He rubs his hand across his head, letting out a loud exhale. "Things just got so messed up."

"You think?" I say with a raise of my brows.

He sighs. "Look, can you just talk to her for us? I know she's not a fan of yours, but it seems like you're the only one she'll talk to right now, so ..." He shrugs.

I shake my head. "If you want to talk to her, do it yourself."

Masie steps forward and laces her fingers with Blaine's. "West, please just tell her to talk to us. We know we messed up, but it's not our faults that we like each other."

"You should've told her," I tell her. "You're her best friend. She shouldn't have found out the way she did."

"I know," she agrees. "But all I can do is apologize. And I can't even do that if she won't talk to me."

"Why do *you* need to apologize?" Blaine asks Masie. "You didn't do anything wrong."

I shake my head in annoyance. "She stabbed Lex in the back."

"It's not Masie's fault Lex likes me." A trace of a smile tugs at his lips. "And honestly, can you blame her? I'm pretty damn hot," he tries to joke. It sets something off inside me. Something that burns underneath my skin.

My hands ball into fists. "Are you being serious right now?"

Blaine holds up his hands in front of him. "Dude, chill. I'm just trying to lighten the mood. Even though I still don't think me or Masie did anything wrong, I know Lex's feelings are hurt, but it's not like I was dating her or anything."

Hearing him call her Lex is what makes me snap.

I take a swing, my knuckles colliding with his jaw.

He stumbles back, landing on his ass and clutching his face. "What the hell is wrong with you, man?" he growls, his face red.

"Jesus, West," Masie breathes out, tears falling from her eyes as she rushes toward Blaine. "Why did you do that?"

I look down at Blaine. "He's an asshole. That's why I did it."

Blaine's lips part to say who the hell knows what, but the door behind him is opened and out steps his dad, dressed for work in his police uniform.

Yeah, did I forget to mention Blaine's dad is a cop?

"What's going on?" he asks as he scrutinizes the three of us.

"West just sucker punched me," Blaine gripes, getting to his feet.

Blaine's dad looks at me then back at his son. "You want me to take him in?"

Blaine looks at me, his eyes cold. "Yeah, I do."

I shake my head, but I'm not surprised. Back in the day, I would've been. But like I said, Blaine's changed a lot over the last year or so.

Blaine's dad gives a nod then turns to me. "Come on, West. If you cooperate, I won't handcuff you."

"I don't give a shit about getting handcuff." No, what I give a shit about is when my dad hears about this later. He's going to kick my ass.

Fuuuck.

As I walk away from the porch beside Blaine's dad, I cast one final glance at Blaine.

"*We're done,*" he mouths.

I give him a thumbs-up. *I totally agree.*

7

WEST

My dad is a well-respected lawyer in town, who has a lot of connections to a lot of very important people, and that's probably why Blaine's dad decides not to haul me into the station. Instead, he drives me home. I'd much rather have gone to the station.

"So, what were you and my son fighting about?" Blaine's dad asks as he steers into the neighborhood where my house is located.

Most of the houses on the street are at least two-stories and have three-car garages. My house is one of the biggest and fanciest, but it's all for show. Everything about my life is.

"A girl," I mutter, trying my best not to breathe through my nose. The stench of the back seat of his patrol car smells like vomit. I'm pretty sure it's coming from a yellow stain on the floor.

"Isn't it always?" He nods understandingly as he turns into my driveway. "My advice is for the both of you to move on from the girl you're fighting over. Your friendship is important to Blaine, and I wouldn't want to see that ruined because of some girl."

Some girl? Lex is definitely not *some girl*. Just like my and Blaine's friendship isn't that important. Just like I know he's more than likely saying this so he can stay on my dad's good side and keep on receiving those big, fat donations my dad writes the police department every year. But I nod anyway, just so he'll stop talking about this. "Yeah, okay."

He smiles then climbs out of the car and opens the door for me.

I climb out, massaging the hand I hit Blaine with.

"I'm going to let you take this from here," Blaine's dad tells me, glancing at the front door as my mother steps out, a look of disappointment on her face. He waves at her then moves to get into the car. "You should put some ice on that hand. It'll keep it from swelling."

I nod. "Okay."

"And you can pick up your car whenever," he adds as he ducks back into his vehicle. "Just as long as you don't pick another fight with my son, understand?"

I nod again, but it takes a lot of effort this time.

I grit my teeth and stand there as he backs out onto the road and drives away. Even when he's long gone, I don't budge.

Maybe if I just stand here, I'll disappear.

"Get inside. Now," my mom snaps, crushing my hopes of sudden invisibility.

Biting down on my tongue hard, I start toward the house. When I reach her, she shoves me inside and smacks the back of my head.

"So, what did you do this time?" she asks, slamming the door behind us.

I shrug. "I punched Blaine. But in my defense, he deserved it."

She glares at me. "Is he going to press charges?"

I shake my head. "I don't think so."

"Good." She smooths her hands over her hair then across the front of her dress. "I have some guests coming over tonight. You can stay in your room. Delilah will bring you dinner."

Delilah is our maid and used to be my nanny until I got older. She's more of a mother to me than my own mother.

I turn for the stairway, confused as to why my mom is letting me off the hook so easily.

"And this isn't over yet," she calls out. "I've got other things to do right now, but later, I'm going to talk to you about this. And you will be punished when your father gets home."

I smash my lips together as my hands begin to tremble at the mention of my dad. I hate that I react this way, hate that I'm so afraid of him, even now at almost eighteen years old. I wish I were stronger. But my mind is filled with memories of my weakest moments and all of them include my dad.

A kick to the stomach, and then he drags me to my bedroom by my hair.

"If you ever embarrass this family like that again, I'll lock you away. Do you understand?" he growls in my face.

I nod, tears streaming down my face.

"Good." Not a single drop of emotion shows on his face or voice as he throws me into my room hard enough that I bang my elbow against the hardwood floor.

More tears burn my eyes as I regret ever accepting Blaine's dare to steal that game. But I didn't think I'd get caught. Turns out, though, almost everyone in this town knows my family and reports back to him with what I do.

And every time they do, I get punished.

I swallow hard at the memory. It was one of the first times my dad kicked me. I was eight years old.

A few days later, Blaine noticed bruises on my side while we were swimming. When he asked what they were from, I lied and said I'd fallen off the trampoline.

It was the first time I had to lie about a wound my father put on me, but it wouldn't be the last.

"Do you understand me, West?" my mom asks in a low tone, tearing me away from the painful memory and slamming be back to a soon-to-be agonizing reality.

I want to tell her no, that I don't understand why my dad has to beat me. But all I do is nod then silently walk up the stairs, knowing there's no use arguing about it.

While my punishment is probably going to be brutal, I don't regret punching Blaine. Partially because I care about Lex and partially because, at this point, I've become numb to my parents' punishments. Maybe that's why I do what I do next. Or perhaps I'm just living up to my reputation of being the piece of shit my parents believe I am.

Whatever the reason, once I get into my room, I send out a text to Holden and Ellis, a couple of guys who I've been hanging out with for the last handful of months. They're a year older than me and no one really knows I hang out with them. Not Blaine. Not my parents. If Blaine knew, he'd probably ask why the hell I was hanging out with a bunch of druggies, if I'd lost my damn mind. And my parents would ask something similar, only their questions would be followed by a punishment.

And while Holden and Ellis get in trouble sometimes, they're not bad guys.

When I hang out with them, I get a break from having to be the upbeat West everyone thinks they know, because there's like this unsaid rule between the three of us that we don't talk about personal shit. Although, I do know a little about Holden and Ellis due to times when we get a little too stoned or drunk and spend a little too much time yammering.

From what I know, Holden grew up in foster homes after his parents abandoned him until he turned eighteen. Then he got his own place on the bad side of town. Rumors are constantly floating around that he's gotten involved with a group that sells drugs, which is true, but he's a decent enough guy despite that. Sure, he's had it rough and is kind of intense, but he's had my back more than Blaine has over the last few months. Plus, I feel like I can just be whenever I'm around him, like I don't have to play some stupid part that I'm not right for.

As for Ellis, he's had it just as rough. His parents were killed when he was younger and, from what I heard, it happened right in front of him. I've never actually asked him about it. He was adopted when he was five, and while he rarely talks about his adoptive parents, I get this weird vibe that something wasn't right with the family that raised him. Not that I've ever asked about that either. I understand not wanting to talk about stuff like that since I sure as hell don't tell people about the shit that goes on in my house. If I did and my dad found out, things would be worse than they already are.

Me: Hey, anyone up for hitting up the skate park? I need to get the hell out of my house.

Holden: Sure. You wanna pick us up or meet us there?

Me: My car's at Blaine's, so we'll have to meet there unless Ellis wants to drive.

Ellis: If I can get my truck started, I can. But why's your car at Blaine's?

Me: I got into a fight with him and his dad hauled my ass home in his cop car.

**Holden: About time you got tired of that
asshole. Please tell me you got a few good
swings in.**

Me: I sucker punched him pretty hard.

**Holden: Man, I wish I had been there to see
that.**

**Ellis: What the heck started the fight? I know
he's been getting on your nerves, but you don't
really get into fights.**

He's right. I haven't got into many fights, although my
parents will tell you differently since they love to blow
everything I do out of proportion.

Me: Because he was treating Lex shittily.

**Holden: Aw, the infamous Lex. The girl
we've heard you talk about, but you never let
her come hang out with us.**

Yeah, as much as I like Ellis and Holden, bringing Lex
into their world that can get questionable sometimes doesn't
seem like a good idea.

**Me: It's not that I don't let her. She just
wouldn't want to … I'm not really her favorite
person.**

**Holden: You always say that, but from what
I've heard, Alexis seems more like us than she
does that asshole she hangs out with all the
time and that blonde girl … I can't remember
her name, but she's a straight-up bitch.**

Me: Her name's Masie and she is a bitch. But Alexis is … complicated. She used to not be as intense, but then her parents died and she changed.

Ellis: I didn't realize her parents died.

Me: It was a car accident.

Ellis: That's really sad.

Me: I know.

The text stream pauses for a beat, and I start to get up to change, when another buzzes through.

Holden: So, have you thought any more about our proposition?

I chew on my bottom lip, unsure of how to reply.

A couple of weeks ago, I was high as a mothereffer while we were all hanging out. I sometimes get a little chatty when I get like that and may have told a little bit more about my shitty homelife than I meant to after they had implied that I had an easy life because I came from a family of wealth.

"Look, I know I've had it easy with some aspects, and I haven't ever had to worry about having a roof over my head and shit like that, but having money doesn't mean my life is some fantastic picnic. My dad's an asshole," I tell them as I lounge back on the torn sofa at Holden's place.

Holden takes a drag off a joint, curiosity sparkling in his eyes. "He yell at you? Or is it darker than that? Come on, rich boy," he mocks with a grin, "tell us all about your shitty life."

I don't take his mocking personally. That's just how Holden is. I kind of like that about him, that he isn't fake like a lot of other people I know.

I waver for a second, knowing I shouldn't tell the truth, because my dad warned me that he'd beat my ass if I ever told anyone what really went on in our house, but my mind is too cloudy to think rationally.

"Darker." I gesture at a bruise on my face. "The asshole did this to me the other day because one of my grades slipped below a B."

"Why does that even matter?" Holden asks, passing me the joint.

I shrug, taking the joint from him then taking a hit. "Because"—I make air quotes—" 'bad grades make me look stupid, which makes our family look stupid.' "

"That's really dumb logic," Ellis mutters as he pops a cap off a beer.

"For sure," I agree, taking another hit. "But he's always worried about how everyone sees him."

"And yet, he doesn't care that they might see that he beats his kid?" Holden asks with a brow raise.

I press my lips together for a beat. "No. He knows I won't tell anyone."

"If you ever tell anyone about this," he once told me, "I'll make sure you can never speak again."

It was right after he beat me so badly that he broke my arm. I learned my lesson that day: Keep silent or end up broken.

Not that I'm not already broken.

"Maybe you can move out," Ellis suggests with a shrug. "Don't you have, like, a trust fund or something?"

I shake my head. "I can't touch that until I'm twenty-one."

"Oh." Frowning, he takes a swig of his beer.

"Well, if you want, you could always come work with us," Holden suggests in a light tone that makes me think he's kidding.

I let out a laugh, but then I catch sight of his expression and realize he's serious.

"Yeah, I don't think I could do that," I tell him. "I mean, my father would do God knows what if he found out I was selling drugs." Plus, while I like to act all tough, the idea of selling drugs scares me.

Holden studies me for a moment then reaches to take the joint from my hand. "Well, if you change your mind, let me know. The boss is always looking for some new incomers that know the town. And you have all those rich people connections, right?"

"Your boss wants to start dealing to rich people?" I question.

He nods. "Rich people can be the best customers. They use the most and always overpay."

I nod like I understand, but I don't. Not really. I mean, sure, I get high sometimes, but I've never dealt. Plus, I'm not really into hardcore drugs, something I'm pretty sure Holden deals. "I'll think about it," I say.

I still haven't really thought about it. Well, not until Holden just brought it up again.

I pause for a moment, trying to figure out what to say to him.

Me: I'm still not sure if I want to.

He doesn't reply right away, so I hurry and change my shirt and shoes and put on a clean T-shirt and some sneakers.

By the time I return to my phone, Holden has replied to let me know that, if I decide I want to accept his offer, let him know. And Ellis has sent a text, letting us know his truck started so he can drive.

I grab my wallet, keys, a joint, and my skateboard. Then I lock my bedroom door and head out onto the balcony attached to my room to sneak out using the tree beside it.

I know I'm going to pay for this later if I get caught, but with my mom entertaining downstairs, there's a chance she might not notice I'm gone.

Sometimes I think she pretends she doesn't have a son. And sometimes I like that she does—my life is less painful when she does.

After I climb down the tree, I use the back gate to sneak out to the front of the house. Then I hurry down the driveway and out onto the sidewalk, slowing down once I reach the end of the block. Breathing out in relief, I plop down on the grass and wait for Ellis to show up.

As I'm digging out my phone, a shadow casts over me. Moments later, boots appear in my line of vision. The toes are dotted with paint and the laces are undone. I scroll my gaze upward, traveling along a pair of long, smooth legs all the way up to a beautiful girl with wildly wavy hair and the saddest eyes I've ever seen.

"What're you doing here?" I ask Alexis. "No, wait. Let me guess. You missed me so much that you tracked me down so you could see my sexy face."

She looks completely out of it, like she's in some sort of trance. But then she blinks, looking down at me, and just like that, her expression turns neutral. I'm starting to notice she's good at that—turning off her emotions. At least on the outside.

She shifts the handle of a backpack higher onto her shoulder. "I didn't track you down. I was just heading ... somewhere and saw you here, and ..." She starts to walk away, but I jump to my feet and snag the sleeve of her flannel.

"Relax, Lex, I'm just messing with you." I let go of her sleeve as she turns to face me. For a fleeting moment, she looks like she's about to burst into tears. "Are you okay?" I ask worriedly.

She nods, her expression lacking all emotion again. "Yeah. Always am."

I pull back, scratching my neck while assessing her, unsure of whether she's telling the truth or not. Maybe she's still upset about Blaine and Masie? I don't know. It feels like there's more to it than that, though.

Her gaze instantly zeroes in on my hand. "What the hell happened to your hand?"

I lift it up in front of my face and cringe at the sight of my knuckles that are swollen to twice its normal size. I was so distracted with getting the hell out of the house that I forgot to ice it. I also should've taken some painkillers since I'll be skating. It's too late now, though, because there's no way in hell I'm going back into that house.

"It's nothing," I lie, lowering my hand to my side. "I just scraped my hand on something."

"It looks like you hit something." She arches her brows. "Or someone."

"What? Are you an expert on punching things or something?" I tease, not wanting to tell her the real reason my hand is hurt.

She lifts a shoulder, scuffing the tip of her boot against the ground. "I've had to throw a few swings before."

"Who the heck have you been fighting?" I ask curiously. "I mean, I know you're a badass, but I haven't heard of you getting into a fight lately."

She shrugs again. "I haven't gotten into a fight lately, but I have punched a few people before."

"True." I give a short pause before admitting, "I may have punched someone in the face."

She inspects me over with those gorgeous eyes of hers. "Who?"

I eye her over as carefully as she is me. "Why do I feel like you already know the answer to that?"

She chews on her bottom lip, the move nearly driving my body mad. "Masie texted me and told me you punched Blaine in the face."

"Oh." I squirm, feeling as though my secret feelings for her have been exposed.

"So, you did do it?" She squints against the fading sunlight as she observes me closely.

I give a casual shrug, hoping I appear calmer than I feel on the outside, hoping she won't see my feelings toward her. "Yeah, but I partly did it because I'm pissed off at him."

"What'd he do to you that's so bad you wanted to punch him?"

Hurt you.

I resist saying the words aloud and try to think of something more clever to say. But all I end up doing is shrugging and saying, "He's been getting on my nerves lately."

She bobs her head up and down. "Seems like a justifiable reason to punch him."

I cock a brow. "Is that sarcasm I detect?"

She dismisses me with a flick of her wrist. "Nah. I'd be a total hypocrite if I judged you for punching someone."

A trace of a smile tugs at my lips, but it fades when I note her frown. "What's up, Lex? You look upset."

"I've looked like that all day."

"I know, but ... is it because of Masie and Blaine?" Because it feels like it might be something else.

Shaking her head, she blows out a frustrated exhale. "I'm just pissed off that Blaine knows about my crush on him. I hate when people know my personal shit, and this ... I wish I could find a way to make her look like a liar. I mean, if I hadn't lost my shit earlier, I probably could've pretended she was, but then I freaked out and took off and now he knows, knows. And I just wish there was a way to make him think I don't like him anymore. Like, I'm over it ..." She trails off, sliding her gaze to me. "Shit, I forgot you were standing there."

"Glad to know I'm invisible to you," I joke, but it really kind of stings.

"That's not what I meant." She offers me an apologetic look. "Sorry."

"You're fine," I say, but all she does is frown. "Lex," I say, wanting to make her feel better. "Tell me what I can do."

She gives me a funny look. "For what?"

I step closer to her. "To make you feel better."

"I'm fine."

"No, you're not. I can tell."

She fiddles with the leather band on her wrist, the one I gave her. "Yeah, I am. Like I said, I'm just irritated because Blaine knows I like him and I hate people knowing my business. Plus, Masie texted me earlier and was being a total bitch about it."

"What?" I pretend to be surprised, but I'm not.

"Yeah, it's pretty messed up." She shrugs then sighs. "I wish I could say I'm surprised, but part of me isn't."

"Me either," I admit, racking my brain for a solution to her problem.

I get the whole not-wanting-people-to-know-about-my-feelings thing. I've liked Lex forever and, in the beginning, no one knew because I was almost always dating someone else. Or, well, hooking up with someone. But then I kind of stopped that, which led to Blaine asking me if I liked her because, apparently, I spent a lot of time staring at her and talking about her. I told him no, but I'm not sure if he believed me.

Anyway, that's not the point. The point is that, when I was dating people, I was able to keep my feelings for Alexis hidden better.

"You could always date someone else," I suggest, even though the idea makes me feel like I want to punch something. Like, say Blaine's face again.

She tilts her head to the side. "What?"

I shrug. "I've done that before and it worked."

Her forehead creases. "Who did you like that you didn't want them to know?"

I shake my head. "There's no way I'm telling you that. I worked too hard to keep it a secret." I wink at her, but the move feels kind of forced.

She grimaces. "I can see why maybe that'd work, but I'm not much of a dater. Plus, no one even wants to date me."

I roll my eyes. God, she's so blind sometimes.

"That's not true at all," I tell her, holding her gaze, hoping she'll see how much I mean my words.

"Yeah, it is." She heaves a heavy sigh. "And even if it weren't, like I said, I'm not much of a dater anyway ... I'm not even in a place to date right now."

I rub my lips together, the wheels in my brain turning.

Don't say it, West. It'll be a disaster.

"You could always date me?" I say then mentally curse myself.

What the hell is wrong with me? I might as well be holding a sign up that reads: *Hey, I'm in love you, and I'm getting desperate.*

Her brows spring upward. "You think *we*, as in you and me"—she motions between us—"should date?"

"Okay, I'm gonna try not to take your shock about that offensively." I put on a grin, but deep down, I'm hurt and pissed off at myself for letting my emotions get the best of me. There's no going back now, though. "Look, it's not that bad of an idea. I know the situation, so I can totally play along. Plus, we agreed earlier to try to be friends."

"Yeah, but this is pretending to be more than friends," she mumbles, sinking her teeth into her bottom lip as she stares at me in a way that makes me actually start to sweat. "But I guess it might work. Just as long as we don't have to kiss or anything like that."

Shit, did she say yes?

I try not to fucking grin. "Trust me. Having to kiss me wouldn't be the downfall of this idea. I'm a fantastic kisser."

She rolls her eyes. "Whatever. It doesn't matter, because there won't be any kissing."

"But then, how are we going to convince people we're actually dating?" I point out.

She crinkles her nose. "I don't know ... We'll figure it out ..." She sighs audibly. "Look, if we're gonna do this, we should probably make a list of rules."

"Rules?" I pout. "That doesn't sound very fun. And since when are you into rules?"

"I'm not." She shifts her weight. "But this seems like it might be a need-rules sort of thing."

"Why?" I ask curiously.

She gives a half-shrug. "Because."

She's being vague, and it has me so damn curious I can barely stand it.

"Because isn't a reason."

She flashes me a cheeky grin. "Yeah, it is, because I just used it as one."

I decide to play her little game, grinning right back. Then I inch toward her, causing confusion to flicker in her eyes. It gives me a twisted sense of satisfaction.

"All right, Alexis Baker, you've got yourself a fake boyfriend." I keep my gaze fixed on her and stick out my hand.

In typical, Lex style, she holds my gaze in an almost challenging way as she places her hand in mine. The look makes me grin, because she's acting like the Lex I know, which means that maybe she's already moving past Blaine.

"Okay, now for the rules ..." She trails off, pulling a face at something behind me.

I start to turn around to see what she's looking at when a cop car pulls up to the side of us. A moment later, Milo climbs out. He used to be best friends with Alexis's older sister Jessamine until she moved out of the country. Of course, that was a few years ago, and now he's a police officer, all decked out in a uniform and everything.

"Dammit," she mumbles with her nose scrunched.

I cast her a sidelong glance. "I'm guessing he's here for you?"

She lifts a shoulder. "I don't know ... Probably."

I bite back a laugh. Damn, that girl gets in more trouble than I do.

Milo rounds the back of the patrol car and steps up in front of Alexis. "Hey, Alexis, I need you to come with me to the station for a bit," he says with reluctance.

Lex crosses her arms and stares him down. "What the hell for?"

He glances down at her shoes then lifts a brow as he looks up at her again. "Because you have paint splattered all over your shoes."

What the hell?

I glance down at her boots. Sure enough, they're dotted with various colors of paint. Not that I know why that means Milo is here to arrest her.

"I didn't realize that was a crime," Alexis quips in a

snarky tone. "Honeyton's really clamping down on crime, huh?"

Milo heaves a weighted sigh. "Please just be cooperative."

"Whatever," she mumbles then stomps toward the vehicle.

"You gonna be okay?" I call out after her.

What the heck did you do, Lex?

She dismisses me with a shrug. "I always am."

I know she's lying. She hasn't been okay since her parents passed away. And while I want to help her, I can't unless she lets me in.

One day, beautiful girl, I'm going to get you to open up to me, I silently vow to myself. Maybe I can try to get her to do it during this whole fake boyfriend thing.

Yeah, I'm liking the sound of that.

Of course, depending on what rules she tries to set, it might be complicated. But I'll just have to work around it. I'm good at working around complicated stuff.

8

ALEXIS

"I'm sorry about this, Alexis," Milo says as he drives down the main road in town and toward the police station.

He had me sit in front and didn't handcuff me. I think it's because he believes he's being nice. But wherever I sit doesn't matter. I'm still being arrested whether I sit in the front or back. And while I pretend not to give a shit, I know this is going to cause drama with Loki. And I've had about enough drama for the day.

"Why are you sorry?" I glance at Milo with my brows raised. "This isn't your fault."

"I know, but ..." He sighs, gripping the steering wheel. "It doesn't feel right hauling you in. I mean, if Jessa knew ..." He clears his throat, growing squirrely, probably at the mention of my oldest sister.

Milo and Jessa used to be best friends until Jessa took

off to live in London. Now they don't speak, always saying they lost touch, but I think there's more to the story than that.

"But yeah, I don't like that I have to do this," Milo mutters under his breath.

"Why do you have to do it, though?" I ask.

While he insinuated earlier that he's hauling me in because of the whole spray-painting incident, he never flat-out said it. So I'm not positive that's the reason. And I want to be positive of what's going on so I can figure out a way to lie my way out of this.

He glances at me. "Don't you already know?"

I shake my head, playing dumb. "Nope. Don't have a clue."

"Alexis," he says in a tolerant tone, "please don't play dumb with me."

I give him my best innocent look. "I'm not playing dumb. I legit don't know."

He searches my face then shakes his head and focuses back on the road. "Someone spotted you spray painting the side of a store today and reported it."

"*What?*" I pretend to be shocked. "I haven't spray-painted anything except for when I'm in art class."

He flicks a pressing glance in my direction. "There's paint on your shoes."

"Yeah, so? I'm an artist. I always have paint all over everything." I lift up my foot. "Some of these paint splatters are, like, from two years ago." Back before my parents died.

Back before everything went to shit. Back before I stopped caring whether things went to shit.

Back before ...

Back before ...

Back before ...

Almost everything became broken.

A tightness pushes up through me, but I swallow hard, pressing down the urge to scream.

I need to get out of here.

Milo releases a quiet sigh as he turns into the police station. "There's also a good chance you were caught on the store's security cameras," he warns as he parks in front of the building and turns off the engine.

I'm not one to get too panicky, but that remark does have me kind of concerned. Still, I play dumb.

"No it didn't, because I didn't do it."

He lets out another sigh then pushes his door open and climbs out. Then he rounds the front of the car, opens the passenger door, and signals for me to get out. I do so calmly and composedly, refusing to freak out and let on that I'm the one who painted on the store. Innocent until proven guilty, right? And until I know the police have real proof that I did it, I'm going to pretend that I didn't.

Of course, when I enter the station behind Milo and spot Loki sitting in one of the chairs near the front desk, that bit of control kind of slips away.

I throw Milo a dirty look. "You called Loki?"

"I did it for your own good ... You shouldn't have to deal

with this alone." He hooks his keys on his beltloop as he approaches Loki, who has his gaze locked on his phone. "And eventually, we would've had to call him anyway, since you're a minor and he's your guardian." He presses his lips together as he regrets saying the last part.

My chest constricts at the reminder, but I shove that feeling right down. I'm honestly getting tired of this shit. These feelings. I want them off.

Right as I manage to shut off everything inside me and wipe my expression clean, Loki glances up from his phone. Anger immediately flickers in his eyes as his gaze locks on me.

Unlike me, Loki is fantastic at showing his emotions. Although, just a handful of years ago, he used to be a pothead who could barely hold a job. Now, he's twenty-two, runs our dad's bookstore, and is the father to a bunch of teenagers because our parents had no one else to leave guardianship to if they died.

Sometimes I feel sorry for him, for getting stuck with all of us. And maybe if I were a better person, I'd stop doing such shitty things that stress him out. But if I stop doing all the shitty things, then I have to feel all the shitty things.

What I really want is for him to just let me go. I'm almost eighteen, almost an adult, and I think it might be time for him to just give up on me. Maybe if I get found guilty for this, it'll push him to that point.

"Hey, Milo." Loki rises to his feet, ignoring me. "Sorry

about this." He rubs the back of his neck. "How much trouble is she in? Should I get a lawyer?"

"You say that like I've already been proven guilty," I say. "But I haven't."

Loki shakes his head but doesn't comment on my remark.

"I'm not sure yet," Milo tells him. "It all depends on if the store owner wants to press charges. You might be able to work out a deal with him. Considering the circumstances, they might be sympathetic. Maybe she can clean up the paint or something."

Loki bobs his head up and down, flicking a glance at me.

I narrow my eyes at him, silently saying, *Don't you dare use Mom and Dad's deaths to get me out of this.*

"First, we should probably make sure she was captured on video," Milo adds with a pressing look. "If she isn't, then there might not even be a case, since the person who called Alexis in wants to remain anonymous. Or well, sent the note."

My brows furrow. "A note?"

Milo glances at me then nods.

My confusion skyrockets. "Why would they send a note?"

He shrugs. "I have no idea. It's honestly kind of strange considering there's a reward, but yeah, here it is."

He takes out a piece of paper from his pocket and shows it to me. Yep, sure enough, scrawled across the paper is note declaring I'm the one behind the paintings.

It's beyond weird and makes me want to find out who it is. Not that I can think of a way to find that out. I want to, though. Boy, do I want to, especially since Jay was lurking around in that area.

Did that asshole turn me in?

"Let's go back to my desk so we can talk about what's next," Milo tells Loki, drawing me from my inner rage.

Nodding, Loki follows Milo into a mess of desks buzzing with ringing phones and officers chatting with each other. When I don't budge, Loki turns around and signals for me to do the same. He also gives me a look, one that he's given me a lot lately. One that lets me know he believes I did this and that I'm in trouble.

And for a brief moment, I feel guilty, which is definitely a new feeling.

9

ALEXIS

We spend the next couple of hours at the station while Milo tries to find a way to prove I didn't do this, that whoever sent the mysterious note was lying. Unfortunately, the store's camera ended up catching me not only spray painting the store but having my meltdown and scraping my palms against the bricks. And the scrapes are still more than visible. While I'm a good liar, once I see the footage, I realize even my best lie isn't going to get me out of this mess.

Luckily, at least according to Loki and Milo, the store owner isn't going to press charges, as long as I repaint the outside of his store.

"But I don't know how to paint a store," I inform Milo after he tells me the deal the store owner offered.

We're sitting at his desk, which is really messy and cluttered. It's weird since he used to be kind of a neat freak.

Loki and he have been drinking coffee and talking about old times while we waited to hear about the footage. Once that information came in, the two of them made up a game plan to call up the store owner and see if he'd strike a deal so I wouldn't get charges pressed against me, which would lead to probation, and probably a lot of hours of it, considering how many times I've been in trouble.

"Really?" Loki's brow arches. "Because, from the footage I just saw, you seemed like you were pretty damn capable."

I bite down on my tongue to avoid snapping at him. "Spray painting on the side of a building and painting an entire building isn't the same thing."

Shaking his head, he picks up a cup of coffee that's on the desk in front of him. "Well, I guess you're going to have to figure it out because we're accepting the deal." He takes a sip then sets the cup back down. "We're not doing the whole court thing again. We've already done it too much, and I'm already on thin ice with Social Services ..." He trails off, his eyes widening, like he didn't mean for that part to slip out.

Before I can say anything, though, he pushes to his feet. "It's late. We're going home." He turns to Milo. "Thanks for helping us out with this. I really appreciate it."

Milo nods, rising to his feet. "Of course."

They shake hands then Loki walks off, not waiting for me, like maybe he doesn't care if I follow.

And maybe he doesn't.

I really don't know at this point.

What I do know is that he's pissed. No, he's more than pissed, which means we're probably going to get into an argument on our way home. And arguments lead to emotions, which makes me want to run out of here and take off.

"Lex," Milo says quietly before I walk off.

I twist back toward him. "What?"

He glances around then leans toward me. "I don't know how, but no one's made the connection from this act of vandalism to the others you've done around town, and no one should have a reason to look any deeper into this, just as long as you stay out trouble from now on. But if you do give someone a reason to look deeper into this and they make the connection, you might end up with a bigger punishment, so just ... be careful."

By *be careful*, I know he means *stop graffitiing*. And while I get what he's saying, the idea of stopping ...

"Okay." The lie burns on my tongue, but I ignore the feeling and walk off, following Loki out the exit doors.

The moment we step outside underneath the stars, panic seizes ahold of me.

I've been caught, which means, for now, I can't do the one thing that was bringing me that sense of peace in this shit-fest of emotions constantly trying to consume me. And with everything going on...

I should just take off. Run. Leave. It's not like me being around is doing anyone any good anyway. I make everyone miserable, including myself. And with the strict leash that's about to be put on me, things are only going to get worse.

"Get in the car," Loki says to me when he notices me lollygagging in the parking lot, staring out at the sidewalk—my escape.

I almost don't listen to him.

I almost leave.

But I don't. Instead I get into the car and open up my photos. While Milo and Loki were distracted, I took the opportunity to take a photo of that note someone sent into the police, telling them I'm the one behind the graffiting. I analyze the photo, trying to see if I recognize the handwriting. It doesn't look familiar, but honestly, I don't really pay enough attention to people's handwriting. But at home, I have a whole box of old yearbooks with signatures it it, so if it's someone I go to school with, I might be able to figure out who told on me.

10

ALEXIS

"Where did you leave your car when Milo picked you up?" Loki asks as he pulls onto the street.

"I was actually walking around," I mutter. "It broke down at Masie's today."

"Okay," he replies in a clipped tone. "I'll get one of my friends to help me tow it home tomorrow then."

I want to say that West was already planning on helping me, but it might be better if Loki and his friend just does it. That way I won't have to go over to Masie's. Plus, with everything that's happened, the reality of the agreement West and I made before I was picked up by Milo is slowly catching up with.

Fake-date West? What the hell was I thinking? Is that really what I want to do?

I'm not sure.

Loki and I sink into silence after that. The longer we sit in quietness, the more I wonder if maybe he's not going to say anything further about what happened. I cross my fingers that's how this is going to go. But I should've known better because, the moment he parks in our driveway, he shuts off the engine and grips the hell out of the steering wheel.

"Goddammit. Goddammit. Goddammit," he curses then smacks his hand against the steering wheel, startling the hell out of me.

While Loki and I may fight, I've never seen him lose his cool like this. It makes guilt twist inside my gut.

"Why do you have to keep doing this shit?" he mutters, clutching the wheel so tightly his knuckles look white in the moonlight trickling through the window.

"Sorry." I mumble, feeling bad, but I'm not sure what to do to fix this.

"No, you're not," Loki mumbles. "If you were, you would've stopped doing this crap a long time ago."

I glance at him and open my mouth to tell him that's not true, but the lie won't leave my lips, so I end up saying nothing.

As silence stretches between us, he shoves open the door. I think he's just going to get out, but all he does is sit in the seat with the door open.

"I know Mom and Dad not being around has been difficult for you, but you need to remember that it's been difficult for everyone." He stares out the window as he speaks, not looking at me. "And while I made a promise to myself not to worry you guys with adult problems, I'm going to break that rule right now because it's the only thing I can think of to maybe get you to stop getting in trouble." He glances at me then, and I get to see all the worry overflowing from his eyes, which makes that guilt inside me constrict tighter in my gut.

"I wasn't exaggerating at the police station. If you keep doing stuff like this and getting arrested, Social Services is not just going to take you away, they're going to take Zhara and Nikoli away, too. Anna's old enough now that she'll be able to stay, but you guys are still minors. And while I'm not sure if you even care about that—care about any of us anymore—I need you to. Because if I lose them, you"—his voice cracks—"and they lose me ..." He doesn't say anything else; just shakes his head and moves to climb out. "I need you to start caring again. And if you can't do that—if you really don't care about us anymore—then try to think about how bad it'd be to live with someone you barely know, in a house that's not where you grew up, with people who don't love you or care about you like we do." With that, he gets out of the car, leaving me sitting by myself in the darkness.

I wonder if he's worried that I'll take off. It's definitely a risk, but either he doesn't care or he's expecting me to do the right thing and come inside.

Part of me wants to run. Take off and sprint into the darkness, letting it swallow me up whole. It'd be easier to do that, to disappear. But his words echo in my mind.

"I need you to start caring again."

"Think about how bad it'd be to live with someone you barely know, in a house that's not where you grew up, with people who don't love you or care about you like we do."

I smash my lips together. It's been a long time since someone said they love and care about me, since our mom and dad died probably.

Now, though, Loki's trying to tell me that part of that love has stayed. But how? With everything I've done, I thought my brothers and sisters would've stopped loving me by now.

It makes me feel even worse. And also makes me want to figure out who got me into trouble so I can get to the bottom of why and make sure there's nothing else they're gonna do to me.

11

ALEXIS

I can't find my box of yearbooks. Then again, my room is a freaking mess, the closet crammed with boxes. I end up going to bed without finding it, but am totally planning on ripping apart my room tomorrow.

So after a night of rest, I wake up, preparing to dive into those boxes when Loki knocks on my bedroom door to give me the details of my punishment.

"I talked to the store owner. You'll start painting the building on Friday," Loki informs me.

"Okay," I tell him, noting the button-down shirt and slacks he's wearing. "Where are you going so earlier? And all dressed up?"

"I have a meeting," is all he says.

I wonder if it has to do with Social Services. I just about ask, but as if sensing where my thoughts are heading, he talks over me.

"I want you to start working at the store a couple of hours a day." He leans against the doorframe with his arms crossed. "And before you start arguing, I want to remind you that you got arrested again last night for vandalism."

I comb my fingers through my hair. "So, working at the store is my punishment?"

He wavers, fiddling with his tie. "For now."

"Okay ... That's kind of vague, though."

"I know. I'm taking this one step at a time. If you do well with working at the store and painting the building, then maybe that'll be it." He pushes away from the doorframe, straightening. "But if you're a pain in the ass about it, I'll tack on more."

Coming from the guy who used to help me and Zhara sneak out of the house so we could go play night tag with the neighborhood kids. And that's only one example of how Loki used to help us break the rules.

Becoming a dad has made him hardcore strict. Well, maybe not hardcore strict, but still ...

"So, make sure to keep that in mind when you feel like rebelling," he adds, his gaze sweeping the bare walls of my room. The used to be covered in my artwork, but I took them all down the day my art teacher told me my work was crap. Maybe I would've put them back up if my mom and I had gone out for that ice cream. But she wasn't alive when it happened.

"Lex," Loki says, and the hesitancy in his voice lets me know I'm not going to like the direction of where this conversation is going. "This whole graffitiing thing ..." He rubs his hand across his face, glancing at my walls again. "It's not about your art, is it? I mean, I know you haven't painted since Mom and Dad died, so I'm wondering"—he shifts his weight—"if this is some sort of replacement for you not painting anymore."

His words are too close to the truth and strike a deep nerve, located in the center of my heart, amongst all those thorns. The strike makes them tighten and pierce my heart, making it hard to breathe and fueling me with frustration.

"No, it's not about anything," I lie. "I just do it because I'm bored and because I don't care."

His throat bobs as he swallows hard. "Lex, I know this has been hard on you, but it's been hard on everyone. And we're all doing whatever we can just to make it through it, but if you keep shutting everyone out like this, that pain you're carrying around is always going to be there. It's not going to heal."

I hate where this conversation is going. He doesn't even know everything. And I won't tell him. Can't.

"If everyone is going through it, then why do you only spend time lecturing me?" I ask Loki. "Why not focus on them instead?"

"I do," he insists. "You're just never around to see it. Plus, Nik and Zhara are dealing with this differently than you are. And Anna did."

"You mean, their way of dealing with it is easier on you?"

"That's not what I said."

"But it's what you think."

He doesn't answer right away, and I can tell he's thinking that Nik and Zhara are the easier ones. And now that Anna's cleaned up her act, she is, too. With Jessa out of the picture, that only leaves me.

"That's not what I think at all," he tries to assure me. "I worry all the time about how quiet Nik's gotten. And Zhara ... she's covering up her feelings by pretending everything's okay, and I know that's not healthy. And one day, I'm worried she's going to break. And Jessa ..." He shakes his head, raking his fingers through his hair. "She barely calls home anymore."

I don't know what to say. I feel like he's letting out stuff that he's been bottling up for a while now. I'm not sure if he even realizes he's doing it.

"I'm sorry," he quickly says. "I shouldn't be talking to you about this."

Then he turns around and leaves, leaving his words echoing in my head. And a lot of guilt. But I quickly become distracted as I receive a text message.

Unknown: Figured out who I am yet?

I grit my teeth as I reply back.

Me: Nope, but I will.

L oki is barely home all day, busying himself with whatever he was doing this morning. I see him for only a brief moment when he tows my car home. He barely says anything to me, just giving me the keys before taking off to the store.

The house stays pretty quiet for the day, and I spend most of the day in search of those box of year books.

I don't get another text from unknown, so I'm hoping I scared them off, but highly doubt it. I haven't heard from West or Masie either, but Blaine does send me a text.

Blaine: Hey, can we talk?

That's all he says, and I don't reply, instead busying myself with rummaging through old boxes.

A lot of the stuff inside the boxes, like old clothes, toys, stuff I wonder why I kept at all. I decide to give the clothes to a donation center and pile them into a bag. Then I move onto the next box that has photos inside of Blaine, Masie, and West, back when we were kids and everything wasn't so complicated.

Blaine was one of the first friends I ever made. We bonded over coloring. He was impressed with how well I could stay in the lines. But what really sealed our friendship was when I shoved down a kid at recess for trying to kiss me and Blaine lied for me so I wouldn't get in trouble. I knew then that he had my back. And I always had his. Until now anyway.

Things started to change the older we got. I became

friends with Masie, and he became friends with West. While we all hung out together, I started hanging out with Masie more, and he did the same with West. But as our friendship changed, I started seeing and feeling differently toward him. When he flirted with girls, I felt jealous. And when I didn't spend a lot of time with him, I found myself missing him. It took me a while, and a conversation with Masie, to realize I was falling in love with him. Or at least that's what I believed.

As I sit here, sifting through these photos, I remember what it felt like to feel that way toward him; how whenever he put his arm around me or smiled, I felt butterflies in my stomach. I also realize those butterflies haven't been there in a while.

I also haven't smiled in a very long time.

Pressing my lips together, I tuck the photos back into the box then stick them on the top shelf where I won't have to acknowledge their existence. Then I move on to the next box in my closet. The moment I look inside, I frown.

My old paintings. And lying on top is the last one I ever painted. The one my teacher told me was generic and unreal. When I had finished it, and before I turned it in, I had thought it was my best work to date. Looking at it now, though—the bright colors, the perfect, flawless lines—I can see what my teacher meant.

"It looks like a freakin' paint by numbers painting. I should just throw all this away," I mutter. "It's not even who I am anymore."

But I can't seem to bring myself to do it, so I end up kicking the box underneath my bed where it's out of sight, but annoyingly, not out of mind.

Of course, the next box I open is the yearbooks so that cheers me up a bit. But then I realize that a lot of people have signed the books on various pages which means I have to look page by page, so yeah, awesome

* * *

I spend a little while looking through the year books before deciding to take a break. I haven't found any handwriting matches, but I also have a couple of yearbooks to look through still.

It's nearing eight o'clock when I wander out of my room to go get some dinner, finding the kitchen strangely empty.

Apparently, Loki isn't home yet.

The door to my twin sister's bedroom is open as I pass by it, and I see her sitting on her bed, just staring off into space, which is strange for her. Usually, she's busying herself with chores, homework, and other do-gooder stuff.

While we're not identical, we used to look similar, except for her hair is shorter than mine and has more wave to it. Her white top and pink shorts get-up would have been something I borrowed. Now pink ... bright colors ... that's not who I am anymore. Just like I'm not the kind of person who talks to their twin sister twenty-four seven anymore.

I have every intention of strolling by her room without

saying a word, but then I remember how she texted me yesterday, about how she needed to tell me something.

"Hey," I say to her while leaning against the doorframe with my arms crossed.

She blinks at me. "Oh, hey." That's all she says, which wouldn't be that strange, except Zhara is the kind of person who can chatter someone's ear off. At least when she's around someone she knows.

"Is everything okay?" I ask cautiously.

She nods then puts on that fake smile I know she wears sometimes when she's trying to lie. "Yeah, I'm totally fine."

Why is she lying?

"You texted me yesterday that you needed to tell me something."

Her brows dip before recognition clicks. Then anxiety creeps across her face. "Oh, I didn't mean to send you that," she babbles in a rush. "I mean, I did, but what I needed to tell you wasn't important and now it's changed, so ..." She shrugs. "Sorry for bugging you. I know how much you hate it when I do that."

Seriously, what the actual hell?

"Dude, are you sure you're okay?" I double-check, eyeing her over. She's acting twitchy and completely unlike herself. Usually, she's more put together.

She bobs her head up and down then stands up and crosses her room that is so pink and glittery that it looks like a faerie vomited all over everything. "Yeah, I'm fine. I need to work on some homework, though, so ..." She gestures for me to move as she reaches to shut the door.

She's dismissing me? Zhara, the girl who can't even tell anyone no, is dismissing me?

"Um ... Okay." I step back, feeling completely out of my element. "Well, if you need to talk, I'll be in my room. Probably for a while after the trouble I got into yesterday."

This would usually be where she starts pressing for details about what I did, which would lead to her lecturing me—that's how it's always been in the past, even before our parents died—so flags start popping up everywhere when all she does is nod and shut the door. Moments later, music starts playing from the other side.

Okay, I guess we're done then.

I turn and head for my room, scratching my head and trying to figure out what in the hell my twin is lying about. I end up passing by my youngest brother's door on my way. It's shut and music is on.

What is this? Teenager Angstville?

Is this how things always are around here? It's been a while since I stayed home for an entire day, so I'm not sure. If so, then no wonder Loki is losing his damn mind. Between my crap and our house turning into Angstville, he probably doesn't have a single drop of fun anymore.

Moving farther down the hallway, I wander into my room and close the door, resisting the urge to turn on some music. Then I stare up at the ceiling, trying to figure out what the hell to do with all this time on my hands.

I painted the ceiling black the day after my parents died, along with the walls, after I got way too stoned.

That day, some a-hole had written *CORPSE GIRL. EVEN YOUR SKIN FEELS LIKE ICE* on my locker in marker. While I didn't have proof, I'm pretty sure it was Jay. Luckily, he was stupid and used washable marker, so it wiped right off. But enough people saw it, and I spent the day feeling like crap.

I was a hot mess of anger and angst, so I ended up getting into a fight with some random person. Knowing I was going to probably get suspended, I took off and started walking all over town to avoid going home. As my anger built, I longed for a canvas and a paint set. That's when I passed a wall covered with graffiti, and a spray paint can just happened to be nearby. Call it fate, but I found myself picking up the can and painting the wall.

After that, I felt better. And that's when my habit started.

My phone suddenly buzzes with an incoming text from Masie, drawing me from my thoughts. I almost don't read it, yet curiosity gets the best of me and I find myself stupidly swiping my finger across the screen.

Masie: Hey, I know you're not talking to me, but there's a party tomorrow, and I'd really like you to come with me. I think it'd be a good chance for us to talk. And maybe you could talk

to Blaine, too. **He misses you, Lex. We both do. You're our friend.**

Friend. It's like she doesn't even know what the word means.

Me: No thanks.

It's all I say. I could say more, say everything I'm feeling, but I don't really want to talk to her. Eventually, though, I'm going to have to face her and Blaine. And while I'm friendless.

Well, maybe not totally friendless, if West and I are still going to try to be friends.

And what about that whole fake boyfriend/girlfriend deal we made? Is that still on? I haven't heard from him since last night when he texted to check up on me and I told him about Milo towing my car home.

Masie sends me another text, but I ignore it and open up a text thread with West. Then I hover my fingers over the buttons as I figure out what to say, other than: *Hey, are we still gonna pretend to date or what?*

I dither. Well, I guess that might work.

Not seeing a better alternative, I type out the text message. Then I put the phone down, assuming it'll take him a while to text back, seeing how it's spring break and late enough that he's probably out partying or whatever it is West does. Honestly, I'm not really sure. Yeah, we hang out and everything, but not enough that I know everything about him. For all I know, he could have this whole other life. I mean, I didn't even know him and Blaine weren't that close anymore. When I really think about it, though, I haven't seen them hang out as much as they used to ...

Wait. Why am I overanalyzing West? What the heck is wrong with me?

I pull a face at the realization, picking up my phone as it buzzes.

Surprise flickers through me when I see West has replied. Honestly, I thought it was going to be another text from Masie.

West: Of course we are. We made a deal and shook on it. And I take handshake deals very seriously.

I roll my eyes. God, he can be such a weirdo sometimes.

Still, seeing that he's still on board with the plan relaxes me a bit.

Me: Okay, cool. We should probably go over the rules, though, and decide how we're gonna do this so it can actually look real. Although, I think some people will probably be a bit skeptical.

West: Why's that?

Me: Um, because anyone who knows us knows there's no way we'd ever date.

West: Yeah, I'm not gonna agree with you on that. I think most people are waiting for us to hook up.

Me: What??? No, they aren't!

West: I've heard a couple of people say it. They think that's why we're always fighting. That it's sexual tension.

I pull a face but can't help thinking about how we bit each other's necks yesterday.

I scratch my forehead, trying not to panic.

West: Did I scare you off? Because I was just kidding. I pinkie promise.

I actually don't think he was, but I don't call him out on it.

Me: We should probably talk about the rules.

A minute ticks by before he replies.

West: Okay, what are they?

Me: Well, I've been thinking about it, and I think there needs to be a no-falling-for-each-other rule. I mean, I really doubt that'll happen, but I don't know. I just want it to be a rule.

West: You know setting rules can't control that sort of stuff, right? Rules can't stop you from feeling stuff.

That's not true at all. At least with me.

Me: I need it to be a rule.

West: Fine. What else?

Me: Well, after this is over, I think we should just go back to being enemies.

West: When were we ever enemies?

Me: Um, since forever. Well, except for yesterday.

West: Maybe. But yesterday we also agreed to try to be friends.

Me: Okay, maybe you're right, but that doesn't mean we've actually become friends yet. And besides, I really doubt we're going to be able to stop arguing all the time.

West: Friends can argue. In fact, it's not a healthy friendship if you don't argue a little bit.

I think about how Blaine and I never argued and almost type it to prove him wrong, but then I remember what happened yesterday.

Were Blaine and I ever really friends?

Me: Okay, how about frenemies?

West: Frenemies with benefits?

Me: Yeah, I'm going back to my original statement of being enemies.

West: I'm just messing with you. You can call us frenemies if you want, but I think you and I are going to be BFFs after all this is over.

Me: Guess you better work on those hair-braiding skills of yours, because my hair's a lot longer and more untamable than Blaine's.

West: I'll get right on that. But you need to

practice our sleepover skills. Because, from what I've heard, you're quite the snorer.

Me: Masie has such a big mouth.

The mention of her makes my chest feel tight, but I clear my throat, trying to clear out the congestion.

Me: But anyway, I'll work on my sleepover skills. But I do think there needs to be one more rule, and I already sort of said it earlier.

West: Aw, the no kissing rule. I remember. I also remember telling you that won't work if we want to look like we're dating.

Yeah, I remember him saying that, too, and while I'm not one to make a big deal out of kissing someone, I also haven't kissed anyone either.

I reread the text as I thrum my fingers against the sides of my legs, trying to figure out how to tell West about this kissing thing without looking like a freak. But then I say to hell with it and decide to type part of the truth.

Me: The kissing thing might be a problem since I've never kissed someone. And I don't think doing it in front of people for the first time and me being all awkward about it is gonna make our relationship look real.

He doesn't respond right away, and I brace myself for some snarky remark to ping through, so I'm shocked by the text he finally sends.

West: If you want, I can come over there and

practice with you. I'm not doing anything right now, except for hanging out with a couple of friends. I know it might be kind of weird, but I think it's better to do it in private.

I have to read the text message twice to make sure I'm understanding it correctly.

He wants to come over tonight and practice kissing?

West and me kissing?

Kissing?

What the actual hell?

Me: Tonight might not be the best night. I'm kind of in trouble right now.

West: I'm glad you brought that up. I wanted to ask you what happened yesterday but didn't know if you wanted to talk about it.

Me: I really don't. Let's just say that I have to spend next weekend repainting the side of a grocery store.

West: So just a usual weekend for you?

I send him the middle finger emoji, and he responds with a cheeky grin emoji.

I'm so close to smiling, and I have no clue what to do with that. Fortunately, he sends another text that distracts me.

West: Maybe I can just come over tonight and sneak into your room. I know you're in trouble and everything, but one of Blaine's foot-

ball friends is having a party tomorrow night and I was thinking it would be the perfect opportunity for us to kind of show up together as a couple.

He's probably talking about the same party Masie invited me to. I don't want to go. At all. But I also know West might be right.

Huh ... I never thought that thought would flow through my mind.

West: Unless you can't go. I'm not sure if you're grounded or not.

Me: Loki never mentioned being grounded.

Not that he's going to be on board with me taking off to a party only forty-eight hours after I get in trouble for vandalism. Still, if I do some good deeds, maybe he'll let me out. If not, I can always climb out the window.

West: So, you think you can come?

Can I?

Do I even want to?

I'm not sure.

I sigh at myself.

Me: I might be able to make it happen.

West: Awesome. Then I'll head over now. Be there in like thirty minutes.

Wait ... What?

Through me trying to figure out if I could go to the party, I forgot the reason we were discussing it.

Panic sets in, and I just about text him to tell him not to come. That we don't need to practice kissing. That I'll wing it. But then I picture myself at the party in front of all those people, and West leans in to kiss me.

Yeah, practicing might be a good idea.

"You can handle this," I try to convince myself.

Even with my mental pep talk, my pulse races as I think about lips, and West's lips, and his tongue piercing I felt on my skin yesterday when he licked my neck. And how, for a very, very small microsecond, it felt ... good?

Yeah, seriously, what the heck is wrong with me?

That's becoming the million dollar question.

Before West gets here, I decide to get something to eat. I head down to the kitchen. Loki has apparently returned home. At least, the empty grocery bags on the counter suggest so. But I haven't seen him, so I'm betting he's up in his room.

Anna, however, is in the kitchen, and so is her friend, Luca.

They don't notice me walk in, because they're whispering to each other about God knows what.

"Just an FYI, you're not alone anymore," I announce as I cross the kitchen and wander over to the fridge.

They jerk back, looking guilty. About what, who knows, and while I'm kind of curious, I'm not enough to ask.

"Hey, Alexis," Luca greets me with a smile.

Instead of answering Luca, I just raise my brows then open the fridge and start digging around for something to eat.

"Hey, if you're hungry, we're heading out right now to get something to eat," Anna tells me.

Just a little while ago, she would've barely registered I existed, partly to be a bitch and partly because she'd more than likely be high. She's different now, though, but I'm not sure why.

"I'm good," I reply, not bothering to mention that I can't go anywhere because West is coming over to practice kissing for our fake relationship. Because, yeah, that'd go over really well.

Anna frowns but quickly recovers with a smile. "Okay. Do you want us to bring you anything back?"

I shake my head, grabbing some stuff out of the fridge to make a sandwich. "I'm good."

She nods. "All right. Well, if you change your mind, text me."

I give her a thumbs-up, then busy myself with making a sandwich as they leave the kitchen.

Ten minutes later, I've eaten and am cleaning up when I receive a text from West.

West: I'm just about there. Do you want me to knock on the door or do you wanna just meet me outside? Not sure if you're allowed to have anyone over or not.

While I'm pretty sure Loki is up in bed, I don't think having West come into the house is a good idea.

Me: Just text me when you get here and I'll come out there.

West: Cool. See you in a few.

He seems so casual about the situation. I wish I was—I try to be—but my heart speeds up as the reality of the situation crashes over me.

He'll be here in a few.

To kiss.

And I'm pretty sure I have lunchmeat stuck in my teeth.

I cup my hand in front of my face to do a breath check then pull a face at the stench.

"Well, that smells lovely," I mutter to myself, deliberating if I want to go brush my teeth or not. It would be kind of funny to kiss him with rancid lunchmeat breath. It'd be a good revenge for all those times he teased me and annoyed the hell out of me. But he was nice to me yesterday ...

"Dammit," I mumble as my conscience gets the better of me again and I drag my butt upstairs to brush my teeth. I don't bother cleaning up or fixing my hair, though. I will not be that girl who gets all fussy about their looks just because a guy is coming over.

By the time I've brushed and rinsed my mouth with mouthwash, my phone is buzzing in my pocket. I fish it out, confused as to why someone is calling. And I become even more confused when I see that it's West calling me.

Maybe he's calling to cancel.

Maybe it's good that he is.

"What's up?" I say, trying to sound more casual than I feel.

"Nothing. I'm just calling to let you know I'm parked out front."

"Oh, okay." But that still doesn't explain why he randomly called instead of texting.

"Why do you sound so confused right now?" he asks curiously.

I lean against the bathroom counter. "It's just weird that you called. I mean, usually we just text."

"Yeah. I know." He gives a short pause. "I just figured it might be a little more gentleman-like of me to call instead of text, considering we're about to make out."

"If you say so." My voice sounds smooth, but I'm a mess on the inside.

Shit is getting real.

"Wow, I thought you'd be impressed by that," he teases.

I roll my eyes, even though he can't see me. "Well, you didn't."

He chuckles. "Damn, I guess I'm going to have to do something more impressive then."

"Why're you trying to impress me at all? This isn't like a date or anything. Just you popping my cherry with this whole kissing thing."

The line grows quiet.

"Hello?" I wonder if he hung up.

"Yeah." He clears his throat. "So, are you gonna come out? Or just keep procrastinating?"

He's acting weird, even for him. *Twitchy*. Like Zhara was earlier.

"Are you sure you still want to do this?" I check. "Because we don't have to." Because I'm not fully sure I can do this.

"Yeah, of course I want to." He sounds uncertain, though, and I'm about to suggest that maybe we don't do this when he says, "Come on, get your cute butt out here. We've got kissing to do." Then he hangs up, giving me no time to back out, as if he knew that's what I was going to do.

And I want to. In fact, maybe I should. Maybe I'm not ready for this. I just found out about Masie and Blaine yesterday. Not to mention I almost got arrested yesterday, too.

No, I'm going to do this. I need to do this.

So, sucking it the hell up, I leave the bathroom to go outside and kiss my frenemy.

12

ALEXIS

West is leaning against the car when I walk out, dressed in black jeans, a matching T-shirt, and black boots. With how dark it is outside, I can barely make most of him out, except for his blond hair that almost looks white against the moonlight. I can't see his expression until I make my way across the front lawn and stop in front of him. Only then do I realize he looks nervous. He also looks a bit tired. Or, well, maybe hungover.

That realization brings a drop of relief to me—that I'm not the only one who's nervous. But then I start to overanalyze the cause behind the nervousness.

Maybe he really doesn't want to do this.

Awkward silence stretches between us, filled up by the chirping of crickets and my next-door neighbor belting out the lyrics to a rock song from his front porch, something he does whenever he's drunk.

"Hey," he greets me with a small smile then offers me the box he's holding. "I brought you something."

Confused, I take it and peer in the box. Inside is a cupcake with vanilla bean frosting. "Thanks. It looks delicious." I glance up at him. "Why'd you bring me this, though?"

He shrugs, stooging his hands into his pockets. "Don't guys normally bring girls flowers when they go out on dates?"

"Some do, but these aren't flowers," I say. "And we're not really going out on a date."

"I know it's not really a date, but it still felt like I should bring you something," he explains. "And you're not really a flowers sort of girl. But you have the biggest sweet tooth ever so I thought a cupcake would be way better."

He's right. I've never really gotten the give-girls-flowers tradition. I mean, seriously what's the point? You get these things that just sit there in a vase until they wither and die. A cupcake however, you devour.

But anyway...

"Thanks," I tell him. "It looks yummy."

He smiles, his gaze briefly flicks to my house before landing back on me. "Can you take a walk with me? Or is that going to get you in trouble?" His lips quirk. "Or should I say more trouble?"

I roll my eyes but relax. I can handle a joking West. It's when he gets nervous that throws me off balance.

"I'm good," I say. "I think Loki's asleep. Honestly, I don't know if he'd even care. He's in one of his moods where he'll barely talk to me. Let me just go set the cupcake down, though."

He nods and I hurry inside and hide the cupcake in a cupboard in the kitchen so no one will find it and eat it. Then I head back outside and West and I start down the sidewalk, heading to who knows where.

"You sure you're not going to get into trouble for leaving?" West double checks.

I nod. "Like I said, Loki's pretty much ignoring me right now."

"I wish my parents would ignore me whenever they got pissed at me," he mumbles.

I walk beside him with my arms wrapped around myself. Goosebumps sprout across my flesh, and while I want to play it o as the air being chilly, the spring air in Fareland is warm and slightly damp.

"Do they yell at you a lot?" I ask as we reach the street corner. "Because your mom doesn't seem like much of a yeller, but you told me once that they yell at each other, so ..."

"She's not much of a yeller." He stares down the road so I can't see his face, but I detect a slight shift in his voice. "She's more of a hand-the-problem-over-to- my-dad sort of person."

I know West well enough to know he's not a huge fan of his dad's. Although, I'm not exactly sure why.

"You and your dad don't get along very well, right?" I ask, stuffing my hands into my pockets.

He shakes his head and starts across the street with me following right beside him. "Not really ... I know everyone in this town thinks he's this great guy, and he is to almost everyone else except his family."

"Yeah, I remember how you told me he treats your mom like shit, that he yells at her all the time." I hop onto the curb as we reach the other side of the road.

He glances at me from the corner of his eye, his expression unreadable. "You know, you're the only person I've ever told that to."

"I think you told me because we were drunk. You get super chatty when you drink too much. Seriously, you're worse than Masie." I flash him a smirk.

His eyes widen in mock shock. "You so did not say that."

I grin. "I totally did. And I'd totally say it again."

He gives me a devious grin. "Yeah, well, at least whenever I see a spider, I don't scream in a more high-pitched voice than Masie does when she's whining. Seriously, it's like you're trying to be her doppelgänger or something."

I blast him with a nasty look. "My scream isn't that high pitched. And spiders are freakin' scary. With all those legs and those eyes and ..." I shudder, just thinking about it, and he totally laughs at me.

I pretend to glare at him then smirk. "Yeah, well, at least I don't freak out whenever I get a zit and almost start crying about it."

"That happened one time," he argues, holding up a finger and biting back a smile. "And I didn't almost cry. I was just annoyed that I got a zit right before my date with Stasha Mellingferd."

"Aw, yeah, the Stasha phase," I remark musingly. "Dude, you were so obsessed with her back in the day."

"Yeah, until I went on a date with her."

"Yeah, what happened with that anyway?" I cast him a sidelong glance. "I mean, she was all you talked about freshman year. Then you finally went on a date with her and never talked about her again. I don't think you two even look at each other anymore." I let a smirk tug at my lips. "It was the zit, wasn't it? Did it like pop on her while you two were making out?"

He pulls a disgusted face. "Hell no! That is just ..." His face contorts with disgust again. "You're seriously so gross sometimes."

I shrug. "Would you rather me act like Masie and be a lady? Because that's not gonna happened."

He shakes his head, strands of hair falling into his eyes. "God no. Don't ever act like her."

I arch my brow. "Even if it means you have to hear me say nasty things?"

He gently nudges my shoulder with his. "I'd rather hear you talk about zits popping than listen to Masie prattle on about her hair and makeup and who's dating who. Whenever she opens her mouth, I feel like I lose some of my brain cells."

"You should hear her talk about shoes," I say as we slow to a stop in front of the park located in the middle of the subdivision.

West stuffs his hands into his pockets. "I'd rather not."

"Yeah, me neither." I waver, considering something. "I guess I won't have to anymore."

As the air between us grows quiet, a bit of pity fills his eyes underneath the moonlight.

I don't want him to look at me that way.

Don't want to be pitied.

I change the subject as I start to squirm. "So, why're we at the park?"

He studies me momentarily before turning his gaze of me and staring out at the swing set and slide. "I just thought this might be the best place to have some privacy while we"—he chews on his lip, his gaze returning to me—"make out."

It's the first time he's said it while I'm standing right here with him. If I thought listening to him talk about it on the phone was uncomfortable, I was wrong.

This is so much more uncomfortable.

"We're not making out," I insist. "Just kissing." But that doesn't sound any better.

Making out or kissing, they both require us to press our lips together. And what even is the difference between kissing and making out? The fact that I don't know makes me seem so lame. God, what I would give to go back in time and not center all my crush energy on a guy who didn't want me. Maybe then I would've kissed someone already and wouldn't be here, about to fake kiss a guy who I've always thought of as a frenemy—

West suddenly presses his lips against mine.

Holy crap. Holy crap. Holy crap.

West is kissing me. His lips are touching mine.

I jerk back, my heart slamming so forcefully that I swear it's going to jump out of my chest and run. And I don't blame it. It's exactly what I want to do.

"Why did you do that?" I ask, cringing at the shakiness of my tone. "You should've warned me before you did it."

He lifts his eyelids and smashes his lips together, taking a beat before answering. "You looked like you were gonna run, and I thought if I warned you that I was going to do it, you would."

"Well, I wasn't," I lie, staring over at the swings and picnic tables to avoid looking at the intensity flowing o him.

"Okay." He sounds doubtful. "Well, at least we got it over with."

I start to relax, turning my head toward him when he steps toward me.

"I'm gonna kiss you," he warns this time, lifting his palm to my cheek.

"Again?" I squeak then hurry and clear my throat. What the hell was that? "But we already did it."

His lips quirk and I expect him to make fun of my squeaking, but all he does is wink at me and say, "That wasn't a kiss, baby."

I quirk a brow and hold up my hands in front of me. "Baby? Are you freakin' kidding me?"

"What?" He gives an innocent shrug. "I'm just practicing for when we start fake dating."

I roll my eyes. "Or you can just call me by my name."

"Sounds good." But his smile lets me know that annoying trait's going to manifest again during out little fake relationship.

He falls silent again, looking at me with a contemplative expression. "I'm going to kiss you again," he says then starts to lean in. "Don't jerk back this time or we're never going to get anywhere."

As he nears my lips, my heart does that stupid thing again where it slams against my chest. I want to move back. I want to run. Yet I find myself remaining motionless as he nears—

I gasp as his lips brush mine then I cringe at the noise, waiting for West to make fun of me. But all he does is release an uneven breath before touching his lips against mine again. He stays that way for a second, and I start to think we're going to keep this strictly a no-frenching thing when he suddenly sweeps his tongue into my mouth. And just like that, West and I are kissing. Or, well, making out, because I'm pretty sure this is different from when he just pressed his lips against mine. That felt more like a kiss.

If you'd asked me earlier if this was how the night was going to go, I would've laughed in your face. I never thought something like this would happen, and part of me thinks I should pull away and end this potential mess right now.

But for some reason, I don't.

My heart is soaring in my chest and my mind is racing so swiftly I can barely think straight. But when West deepens the kiss, slipping his fingers through my hair, all my thoughts just sort of float away. Then he presses his other hand against my back and pulls me closer, kissing me even deeper. Suddenly, I realize that, like spray-painting, kissing can also be a great mind distracter. All I can think about is his tongue tangling with mine, the heat of his body as he gently presses me against him, and how good it feels as he plays with my hair.

This isn't as scary as I thought.

I get so lost in all the sensations that I'm not even aware that he moves us farther into the park until my back bumps against the edge of something.

I startle, slightly pulling away and glancing behind me, realizing I'm now standing by a picnic table.

Confused, I twist back to face him, about to ask him why he moved us over here. But before I can get words to leave my tingling lips, he wraps his hands around my waist, picks me up, and sets me down on the table. Then he moves between my legs and seals his lips to mine again. I kiss him back, my hands unconsciously wandering to his shoulders as I grip on to him and bite his bottom lip between my teeth.

I don't even know what drives me to do it, but I assume he likes it since he lets out a soft moan. Then he urges me closer to him, returning one of his hands to my hair again, combing through the strands until my head tips back. Then he moves his lips from mine to trail kisses down my chin to my neck.

I stare up at the stars, my mind racing, but a cloud of confusion muddles the thoughts. I can't think of anything but the way his lips travel across my neck, the way he gently grazing his teeth along my skin—

My phone buzzes from inside my pocket. At first, I ignore it as West returns his lips to mine. But then it buzzes again. And again.

Sucking back a shaky breath, I pull back, my insides feeling all jittery, like I just drank too much coffee.

Reality quickly settles in as my phone continues to go off in my pocket.

Oh my God, I just made out with West!

West slowly opens his eyes, little airy breaths leaving his lips. "Everything okay?" He seems uncertain again, which is weird since he seemed so confident while he was kissing me. In fact, he basically did everything.

God, I'm so lame.

"Yeah, my phone's just going crazy," I say with a shrug, luckily managing not to sound as shaky as I feel.

Struggling to breathe evenly, I dig my phone out, telling myself to get it together. That it was just a kiss. No big deal. And it was a fake kiss at that.

My fingers tremble a bit as I tap open my text messages.

"Is it Loki?" West asks, playing with strands of my hair absentmindedly.

I might overanalyze how weird it is that he still has his hand in my hair if it weren't for the texts on my phone.

Unknown: I know a secret of yours.

Unknown: And it's not about your crush on Blaine.

Unknown: It has to do with all those pretty paintings you've been putting up all over town.

Unknown: Did you enjoy getting in trouble for the one last night? Maybe I should turn you in for all your artwork.

I swallow hard as I read the texts. So this is the person who turned me in? The person who wrote that mysterious note?

But who is it? Again, that's what I need to figure out.

Although, that might not be my only problem since I think West just saw the texts.

My suspicions are confirmed when he cocks a brow at me. "So, you are the one who's been doing that."

I swallow hard. "You sound like you already guessed that." How, I don't have a damn clue, but it makes me nervous.

I gently push him back, hop off the table, and start to walk o.

He rushes after me, his boots thudding against the grass.

"Lex, chill. I'm not going to tell anyone."

I pick up my pace. "I'm not worried you're going to." No, I'm worried whoever this unknown person is will, and then I'll end up in bigger trouble, like Milo warned me.

I quicken my pace even more, practically running, but he captures the back of my shirt, pulling me to a stop.

"Then why are you running away from me?" He drops his hand from my shirt as I turn toward him with my arms crossed. "I'm not running away," I inform him. "We did our practice kiss, and now I'm leaving so I can figure out who the hell this asshole is that is ... Well, I'm not really sure what they're trying to do, but I'm going to find out, and then I'm going to kick their ass."

"You want me to help you?" he offers, scratching his wrist.

"No, I can handle it." I spin around to leave, but he gently wraps his fingers around my wrist and moves up beside me, catching my gaze.

"Let me help you, okay?" The edges of his lips quirk. "It'll give us something to do while we're fake dating. You know, between all the kissing."

"There won't be that much kissing," I stress. But just the mention of kissing gets my heart racing a bit. It's such a little dumbass.

"Okay." But his eyes glint with amusement. "Then I guess we really need something else to fill up the time, so let me help you with this."

I'm not one for accepting help, but I do want to know

who keeps texting me so I can make sure they keep their mouth shut.

No one else can find out I'm behind those spray-painted words all over town. There's too much at risk if word gets out. My family could get broken up. Plus, everyone would know the real me, the girl behind the mask.

"Fine," I give in, surprising him and myself. He probably thought I was going to be harder to persuade. Honestly, so did I, but I must be really worried. "But how do we even attempt to figure out who this person is? Because so far all I can think of is comparing handwriting to my yearbook and that'll only work if the person doing this is from our school."

His brows dip. "Handwriting?"

Oh yeah, I didn't mention the note to him yet. "Yeah, the person who did this also sent a note to the police ratting me out for that graffiti thing. And while I'm not sure, I'm wondering if it's someone go to school with so I've been going through my old yearbooks to compare the handwriting. So far, though, I haven't found anything."

"That's not a bad idea." He contemplates this with his teeth sunken into his bottom lip. "If that doesn't work, I think we should start out by making a list of the people you think might be doing it," he finally says. "And then go start looking into each of them."

I nod. "Yeah, okay. Well, Masie and Blaine are on that list, even though their handwriting doesn't match the note. But Masie could've gotten someone to write the note for her so I wouldn't recognize it," I tell him.

Jay and his friends are also on the list, but I don't tell him that since that'll lead to a whole pathetic story of just how badly they've tormented me over the years.

His brows elevate in surprise. "Really?"

I nod. "Yeah. I mean, I don't really think they did it, but with how upset Masie was about you punching Blaine and how I didn't care ... And then she was trying to make up with me, but I ignored her ... I wouldn't put it past her to do something like this if she somehow found out I was behind the spray paint. Although, I'm not sure how she got an unknown number."

He wavers his head from side to side. "I really doubt it's them, but I think you should put them on the list just to be safe."

"Okay ..." I chew on my bottom lip. "Why did you seem so surprised when I suggested it was them?"

He gives a half-shrug, staring out at the street. "I don't know. I guess I'm just used to you being"—he shrugs again, looking at me—"team Blaine and team Masie."

"Yeah, but never team Blaine and Masie," I stress. "And besides, I'm over that."

Am I, though? Can you just get over a friendship like that? Maybe. Maybe not. I really don't want to think about it, though. No, what I want is to focus on something else. In fact, I think I'm going to put all my energy into figuring this out.

Although, if this person does turn me in, I might be thinking about some major things. Like probation and whether or not Social Services is going to come yank me and my brother and sister out of our home.

Shit. I need to figure this out, no matter what it takes. Even if it means swallowing my pride and asking West for help. Yeah, he already offered, but I need to make sure we'll get to the bottom of this quickly.

"Hey, West," I say as we start wandering back in the direction of my house.

He blinks at me, seeming sort of dazed. "Yeah?"

"I need to make sure we figure out who this is as quickly as possible and make sure they stay quiet ... It's really important."

He offers me a small smile. "We will." Then, to give me extra reassurance—at least that's why I assume he does it—he reaches over and hitches his pinkie with mine. "I pinkie swear on my life, baby."

I shake my head, wanting to get annoyed at the baby remark, but his pinkie promise has a trace of a smile pulling at my lips.

Blaine, Masie, him, and I used to make these promises to each other all the time, way back in the Before when things were simple. And for a fleeting moment, right after he says it with his pinkie hitched with mine, I feel like everything might work out.

***

When I arrive home, I say goodbye to West then pour

myself a cup of coffee so I can stay awake and finish searching through the yearbooks. I also grab the cupcake, which has vanilla bean frosting on it and is so yummy.

About an hour later, I'm almost finished and haven't been able to match up the handwriting. I'm just about to come to the conclusion that no one from my school wrote this note when I spot it. A match.

And just like that, the mystery behind the note is solved. But it doesn't make things any clearer. In fact, I'm more confused than I was before.

The note was written by Charlotte Melorford who was a senior when I was a freshman. I think she may have been friends with Loki once and that's why she signed my yearbook. But the handwriting is definitely a match. Still, why would she do this? And how did she know I was the one behind the painting?

Confused, I do an online search of her name. And just like that, my puzzlement deepens. Because the first thing that pops up is a missing person's case for her.

Charlotte Melorfod has been missing for a while. But even weirder, she went missing the day my parents died. Coincidence or not, I'm not sure. I'm going to find out, though, no matter what it takes, something I vow to myself when I receive another text.

Unknown: You're going to do what I say, or everyone will find out about your little extracurricular activities.

I reread the message. "This is blackmail."

Just the idea of being blackmailed makes my jaw tick. I want to send the texter a middle finger emoji, but I also don't want everyone finding out that I'm the one who's been graffitiing quotes on buildings all over town.

"How the hell am I going to figure this out?" I mutter.

West offered to help me figure this out, but that was before I become aware that the sender could be connected to a girl that's been missing. But she was also eighteen when she went missing so maybe she just took o. I mean, from what I briefly read online, there wasn't a lot of evidence for the police to look into and some of them believed she might have just taken off on her own. Not that I believe that. I've seen enough crimes shows to know that sometimes police just automatically assume that with cases like the. Although, Charlotte is alive enough to write a note. But the question is: why. What does this sender want from me? And how are they connected to Charlotte?

Hmmm...

I toss my phone aside and march into the closet, going up to the whiteboard that I hung up in there once to doodle on. Then I grab a marker and write in the center of the whiteboard: Look into Charlotte Melorfod.

It's a starting point to what I hope will lead me to some answers. I just hope I know what I'm doing. I mean, sure I've read a lot of detective books and watched a lot of shows. But that doesn't mean I'm going to be able to track down some missing woman. I'm not a detective.

But I'm sure as damn well gonna try.

13

WEST

Lex and I stay fairly quiet during the walk back to her house. Normally, I'd try to fill in the silence by joking around, but my mind is crammed with other stuff right now. Like who could be texting Lex. What their game is. How I'll find all this out, because I will. I take my pinkie promises very seriously. At least with her.

I also can't stop thinking about that kiss ... replaying it in my head ... The way she tasted, how soft her skin was, the little gasps that kept escaping her lips as I gently tugged on her hair, the way she bit my lip. The latter was completely unexpected and totally turned me on. All of it—she did. I just wish the kiss had been real; wish she'd actually wanted to kiss me to begin with.

Still, the kiss was amazing, and I'm going to keep replaying it in my head over and over again until our next one. And maybe, just maybe, along the goddamn way, she'll finally start seeing me as more than a friend. Although, depending on what happens when I get home, I might not be able to leave my house for a while.

I officially haven't been home for more than twenty-four hours. Last night, while I was at the party with Holden and Ellis, my mom started texting me relentlessly with threats, warning me that, if I didn't get my ass home, I was in even more trouble than I already was. Part of me wanted to leave; knew the longer I stayed and disobeyed, the worse trouble I'd be in. But I was too high and drunk, and Holden was introducing me to all these people... I just sort of lost track of time as everything passed by in a haze.

Maybe it was a stupid decision to go to the party at all. But at the time, I convinced myself that I was going to avoid getting my ass beat. But that avoidance has made the punishment pile and fester. And honestly, I'm worried about what'll happen when I get home.

And here I am, promising Lex that I'll help her. What if I can't? What if he makes it so I can't? What if he finally goes through with his threats of finishing me off and putting me out of my misery?

Those thoughts continue to haunt my hungover mind until we arrive at Lex's house.

She starts across the grass toward the front door, muttering a goodbye. If I didn't know her as well as I did, I'd take it personally that she's so eager to bolt from me right after we shared that hot as hell kiss. But Alexis has never been one for facing emotional stuff head-on, even back before her parents died. Although she wasn't as shut off as she is now.

"Hey, Lex," I call out to her.

She pauses then turns around, sucking her bottom lip between her teeth. "Yeah?"

My gaze fleetingly drops to her lips and, damn, I want to kiss her again so badly, but her guarded expression lets me know she'd more than likely kick me in the balls if I tried.

I cautiously step toward her. "I'm going to look into this texting thing and see if there's any way we can find out whose number it is. I have a friend who's really into technology, and he might know something. His name is Ellis, and he's pretty cool, so you don't have to worry about him telling anyone anything."

She bobs her head up and down, nibbling on her lip. "Okay. And I'll get working on my list." She turns to walk up the stairs, trying to bolt.

"Lex," I call out again, my nerves surfacing as I prepare to say what I need to say next.

She sighs heavily then turns to face me. "Whatever it is, West, just spit it out. This whole tiptoeing-around-it thing doesn't suit you." She smirks. "You're too big of a loud-mouth for that."

And just like that, I relax for a moment, reducing the last of the distance between us.

"I was just going to say that I'll text you tomorrow so we can figure out what time we want to show up at the party together." I just hope I'll be able to get out of the house to go to it.

Maybe I just won't ever go home again ...

God, if only ...

"Oh." A crease forms between her brows. "Why did you seem so weird about saying that?"

"I wasn't," I lie. I was, as she put it, "tiptoeing around it," for a ton of different reasons.

She eyes me over so closely I almost squirm. "I can tell you're lying, but I'm gonna let it go for now 'cause I'm tired."

I grin at her, and for a moment, everything is so easy, so weightless. "If I was lying, you'd never be able to get the truth out of me if I didn't want you to."

She rolls her eyes. "Okay. Tell that to Blaine and the many secrets you've accidentally confessed to me about him. Like the time he peed his pants in eighth grade when he was watching *SpongeBob* and laughed too hard."

"Hey," I hiss through a chuckle. "You promised you wouldn't tell anyone."

She crosses her arms. "And I haven't. I'm just making a point that, if I want to get the truth from you, I totally can."

I can't help smiling at her sassiness. "Fine, maybe you're right."

The front porch light flips on then, and she tenses.

"Shit. I better get inside." She reels around and rushes up the steps.

I don't budge until she's safely inside. Then I turn and

head toward my car, the weightlessness dissipating as I face the inevitable, opening up the text messages I've been ignoring.

I have a ton from my mom. None from my dad, though, but that's typical. He never verbalizes anything to me. No, he expresses his words through violence.

Blowing out a shaky breath, I read the last text my mom sent me.

Mom: You'll regret this if you don't get home right now.

The text was sent this morning. More than likely, my parents stayed busy with work and socializing throughout the day. Hopefully, they'll still be busy when I get home. Maybe I'll be able to procrastinate my punishment until tomorrow.

Me: Sorry. I'm heading home right now.

I move to open my car door but pause as she replies back.

Mom: Don't bother. You turn eighteen in a few weeks in a handful of months so you can take care of yourself.

My heart thunders in my chest.

What?

Me: You're kicking me out?

She doesn't respond right away, so I slide into the driver's seat, shut the door, and start the engine. If what she's saying is true, then I ... I really don't know how I feel about it. On one hand, I feel kind of relieved, but on the other …

Where will I go?

Mom: Not so much as kicking you out than you've just decided to grow up and start taking care of yourself because you want to be mature.

I shake my head as I reply.

Me: So that's what you're going to tell everyone, I'm assuming.

Mom: Yep, and you'll play along with the story or there will be consequences. And I don't need to say what those consequences are. You've had them since you were five, so you know the drill. I just wish you were smart enough to realize that if you stopped doing stupid things, you wouldn't have to be punished at all. But clearly, you're not that bright.

I swallow hard at her words. While my dad is usually the asshole, my mother does have her shining moments.

Still, if they kick me out …

Me: What could you possibly do to me if you kick me out? I won't be under your roof anymore.

It's a bold move, at least for the West who lives under that roof. Everyone who knows me outside thinks I'm a bold, blunt guy. But in that house, I am weak. In that house,

I've been beaten down into almost nothing. A ghost. I'm a ghost in that house.

Mom: Oh, there's a lot we can do to you. Your father owns this town, and he and I can make your life a living hell. You need a job? We'll make sure no one hires you. You want a scholarship? We'll make sure that doesn't happen. And you'll need those things because we won't be supporting you financially anymore.

I ball my hands into fists until my fingernails cut through my flesh. So that's their big plan. Take everything away from me.

Me: Why are you doing this to me? I know I messed up but taking everything away from me seems harsh. And someone could find out.

Mom: What happened last night was the end of a very long list of your screw-ups. Your father and I have been talking about doing this for a very long time, and tonight, when your father announced he's running for mayor, we officially decided that it was time to clean up the trash in the family. Starting with our disappointment of a son.

Rage and pain wave through me, making it difficult to breathe. This night had been amazing but is quickly shattering. All those years I spent in that house, letting my dad smack me around, letting my mom verbally abuse me, I did it with the hope that one day I'd graduate and get to take off for college. I had a college fund, a future. Now I have nothing. And the sad part of it is that, even with all that, part of me feels relieved that I finally get to escape from that hellhole that I had called home.

Me: Do I at least get to pick up my stuff?

Mom: I already put your stuff out on the porch. You can pick it up tonight, and then you can meet your dad and me for breakfast tomorrow so you can inform us of your future plans on how you'll take care of yourself. And you better have a good plan. If you don't, like I said, we'll make your life a living hell.

I want to say: *More than you already have?* But I'm too tired. And hungover. And worried about what the hell I'm going to do.

Me: Okay.

That's all I say before I toss my phone aside and grip the steering wheel to drive forward to pick up my stuff. I'm not sure where I'll go after that. I have some money in my wallet, enough to maybe get a hotel room for a week or so. After that, I'm going to end up homeless. But I guess I can live in my car, since the title is in my name, so my parents can't take that away.

It was actually a present from my grandfather. He gave it to me on my sixteenth birthday. He passed away not too long after that. He was the only adult in my life that I ever felt cared about me, and when he died, I felt like a part of me died.

If he were here, I could turn to him for help. But he's not. No one is. I have no one to turn to. Not even Blaine, since we declared our friendship is over last night. Plus, I never told him anything about my messed-up home-life. Lex knows a little about it, but I'm not about to turn to her for help. She has her own problems and doesn't need mine piled onto hers. The only other people who know anything about what goes on in that house are Holden and Ellis. And while they might let me crash on their couch for a couple of days, they don't have a bunch of extra cash lying around, so they can't support my soon-to-be broke ass.

Still, maybe I can crash there for the night.

I steer into a nearby gas station then take out my phone.

Me: Hey, can I crash at your place tonight? My parents kicked me out and I have nowhere else to go.

It takes him a moment to reply, and I grow worried he won't, but then he finally texts back.

Holden: Yeah, that's cool. Just a heads-up, though, my boss is over and we're talking shop. I've mentioned you a couple of times, so he might try to convince you to work for him. I know you've said you don't want to, but it kind

of sounds like maybe your mind could be changed now. Like you might need the money.**

I'm unsure of how to reply. While I'm all for rebelling, dealing drugs instead of occasionally doing them is an entirely different level of trouble.

But he's right. I do need the money. And I really don't have much to lose anymore. Not really anyway.

I'm all alone.

Swallowing hard, I type a reply.

Me: ***Yeah, okay. See you in a bit.***

I'm not sure what just happened, but it feels like maybe I agreed to something. I should be more worried, but honestly, I just feel lost, like Alexis painted on the wall. Drowning in a sea of agony, fighting against the waves.

At this point, part of me kind of wants to stop fighting.

ABOUT THE AUTHOR

Jessica Sorensen is a *New York Times* and *USA Today* bestselling author who lives in the snowy mountains of Wyoming. When she's not writing, she spends her time reading and hanging out with her family.

<u>**Rebels & Misfits Detectives:**</u>

The Confessions of Luna

Untitled (coming soon)

<u>**Guardian Academy Series:**</u>

Entranced

Entangled

Enchanted

Entice

Charmed

Untitled (coming soon)

<u>**Monster Academy for the Magical:**</u>

Monster Academy for the Magical

Monster Academy for the Magical: The Deadly Four

Monster Academy for the Magical: The Monster Trial

Monster Academy for the Magical: The Monster Clique

Untitled (coming soon)

<u>**Harlynn's Mystery Investigations:**</u>

Sugar Cookies & Zombie Secrets

Untitled (coming soon)

<u>**Lexi Ashford Series:**</u>

The Diary of Lexi Ashford

The Diary of Lexi Ashford: The Agreement

Untitled (coming soon)

Enchanted Detectives Series:

Enchanted Chaos

Charmed Chaos

Entangled Chaos (coming soon)

My Cursed Superhero Life:

Cursed

Untitled (coming soon)

The Honeyton Mysteries:

Chasing Hadley

The Deal & a Secret

Untitled (coming soon)

The Heartbreaker Society:

The Mysteriously Complicated Life of Ashlynn: Volume 1

The Mysteriously Complicated Life of Ashlynn: Volume 2

The Mysteriously Complicated Life of Ashlynn: Volume 3 (coming soon)

Tangled Realms:

Forever Violet

Untitled (coming soon)

Curse of the Vampire Queen:

Tempting Raven

Enchanting Raven

Alluring Raven

Untitled (coming soon)

The Unraveling Mysteries Series:

The Mysterious Guy Next Door

The Mystery of the Symbol

Untitled (coming soon)

The Raven Four:

A Pact Between the Forgotten

The Ravens & the Mysterious Town

Secrets Hidden in Dark Places

Untitled (coming soon)

A Pact Between the Forgotten:

The Art of Being Friends

The Rules of Being Friends (coming soon)

Shadow Cove Series:

What Lies in the Darkness

What Lies in the Dark

Untitled (coming soon)

Mystic Willow Bay Series:

The Secret Life of a Witch

Broken Magic

Stolen Kisses

One Wild, Crazy, Zombie Night

Magical Whispers & the Undead

Untitled (coming soon)

Standalones:

The Forgotten Girl

The Coincidence Series:

The Coincidence of Callie and Kayden

The Redemption of Callie and Kayden

The Destiny of Violet and Luke

The Probability of Violet and Luke

The Certainty of Violet and Luke

The Resolution of Callie and Kayden

Seth & Greyson

The Coincidence Mysteries:

The Evermore

Untitled (coming soon)

The Secret Series:

The Prelude of Ella and Micha

The Secret of Ella and Micha

The Forever of Ella and Micha

The Temptation of Lila and Ethan

The Ever After of Ella and Micha

Lila and Ethan: Forever and Always

Ella and Micha: Infinitely and Always

The Secret Star Grove Mysteries:

The Secret Grove Mysteries: Road Trip Interrupted

Untitled (coming soon)

The Shattered Promises Series:

Shattered Promises

Fractured Souls

Unbroken

Broken Visions

Scattered Ashes

Breaking Nova Series:

Breaking Nova

Saving Quinton

Delilah: The Making of Red

Nova and Quinton: No Regrets

Tristan: Finding Hope

Wreck Me

Ruin Me

The Fallen Star Series:

The Fallen Star

The Underworld

The Vision

The Promise

The Lost Soul

The Evanescence

The Mist of Stars (untitled)

The Darkness Falls Series:

Darkness Falls

Darkness Breaks

Darkness Fades

The Death Collectors Series (NA and YA):

Ember X and Ember

Cinder X and Cinder

Spark X and Spark